It was decided.

He and Maggie would be guardians to his orphaned nieces and nephews.

But doubt assailed Trent once again. How would he deal with Maggie?

He'd loved his wife so deeply, and yet he'd been unable to give her what she wanted most: children. And that dream had proved more important than their love.

But now she'll have both, a voice within him whispered. And you can have her back.

Trent ached to be able to forget his anguish in Maggie's arms. But the day she'd left with tears in her eyes, he'd sworn never again to open his heart to that kind of pain. And never to inflict it on Maggie, either.

Because Trent was afraid.

And he was right to be.

Because now he found he had no idea how to be a loving parent....

Books by Kate Welsh

Love Inspired

For the Sake of Her Child #39
Never Lie to an Angel #69
A Family for Christmas #83

KATE WELSH

A two-time winner of Romance Writers of America's coveted Golden Heart Award, Kate lives in suburban Philadelphia with her husband of twenty-six years. She has two daughters whose childhood antics often wind up in her stories. Besides her writing career, Kate works part-time as a graphic artist and does administrative work for an international manufacturer.

As a child she was often the "script writer" in neighborhood games of make-believe. Kate turned back to storytelling when her husband challenged her to write down the stories in her head. With Jesus so much a part of her life, Kate found it natural to incorporate Him into her writing. Her goal is to entertain her readers with wholesome stories of the love between two people the Lord has brought together and to teach His truths while she entertains.

A Family for Christmas
Kate Welsh

Love Inspired®

Published by Steeple Hill Books™

STEEPLE HILL BOOKS

ISBN 0-373-87083-3

A FAMILY FOR CHRISTMAS

Copyright © 1999 by Kate Welsh

All rights reserved. Except for use in any review, the reproduction or utilization of this work in whole or in part in any form by any electronic, mechanical or other means, now known or hereafter invented, including xerography, photocopying and recording, or in any information storage or retrieval system, is forbidden without the written permission of the editorial office, Steeple Hill Books, 300 East 42nd Street, New York, NY 10017 U.S.A.

All characters in this book have no existence outside the imagination of the author and have no relation whatsoever to anyone bearing the same name or names. They are not even distantly inspired by any individual known or unknown to the author, and all incidents are pure invention.

This edition published by arrangement with Steeple Hill Books.

® and TM are trademarks of Steeple Hill Books, used under license. Trademarks indicated with ® are registered in the United States Patent and Trademark Office, the Canadian Trade Marks Office and in other countries.

Visit us at www.steeplehill.com

Printed in U.S.A.

For God so loved the world, that he gave his only begotten Son, that whosoever believeth in him should not perish, but have everlasting life. For God sent not his Son into the world to condemn the world; but that the world through him might be saved.

—*John* 3:16-17

Leona, I couldn't write a Christmas book and not think of you. Thank you for all those extra years you kept me believing in Santa, for the camaraderie during the Great Tree Hunts and on Christmas Eves when we couldn't get to sleep, and for all the years when making Christmas special for the whole family couldn't have been easy but you did it anyway. Most of all, thanks for being my big sister. Oh, and I hope you appreciate that the painting gets finished *before* Thanksgiving. Ain't fiction great!

Chapter One

"There's a Mr. Edward Hanson to see you, Mrs. Osborne. He says it's urgent that he speak to you."

Maggie stared at her secretary. What could Trent's lawyer have to say that would be urgent? Hope flared to life in her heart. Could this be the Lord's answer to prayer? she wondered. Had Trent rethought the idea of divorce as she'd begged him to do?

The flame of hope flickered and dimmed a bit. Were that the case, Trent would have come himself. Just last week hadn't he said he wouldn't change his mind? He'd even asked her not to contact him again. He'd reminded her that he was dating. He was marvelously happy with his life the way it was. The past was past, he'd said. His future lay ahead.

Without her.

And losing him was all her fault.

"Show him in, Connie." She forced a smile, her heartache too personal to share with a co-worker.

"Oh…okay," Connie said, clearly surprised at the break in policy.

Having cut her hours, Maggie's appointments were carefully scheduled now. Forty to forty-five hours a week. That was all she'd ever give to a career again.

Maggie watched Connie's wide retreating back for a few short seconds, then she closed her eyes. *Please Lord. Let this be good news. Bless my marriage. Bring Trent back to me.*

Maggie stood to greet Ed Hanson. His sandy hair was in its usual disarray, his jacket wrinkled as always. He was a man she'd once considered a friend, though he'd been Trent's friend since childhood. And like most of their friends, he had chosen sides in the divorce—Trent's side.

"Ed, good to see you. Won't you have a seat? Can Connie get you something? A cup of coffee? Iced tea or a soft dri—" Maggie's breath hitched in her throat when she saw the desolate expression in Ed's pale blue eyes. Her hand came up to cover her heart. "What's wrong? Is it Trent? Has something happened to him?"

Ed shook his head. "It's Sarah and Michael. And the kids. They were on vacation."

"Yes, I know. Sarah and Michael have remained friends. We attend the same church now. In fact, they—" She stopped. She was babbling. Her heart clenched with fear. "What's happened?"

This time Ed's eyes clouded with tears that he blinked back. Maggie instinctively sank into her chair as Ed began his explanation. "They apparently almost made it to their destination. Two more exits and they'd have been fine. But they didn't make it. Their van was hit by an eighteen-wheeler. The police say the driver fell asleep at the wheel.''

"How badly are they hurt?'' Maggie demanded, on her feet once again.

"Sit down, Maggie,'' Ed said, his tone sad and frighteningly kind.

"Why?'' Her voice shook. "Why must I sit down?''

"Because it isn't good. Not good at all.'' Ed took a slow deep breath. "There's no easy way to say this. Sarah was killed instantly. Michael only lasted an hour.''

"Lord, give me strength,'' Maggie prayed, and once again her fledgling faith did give her the strength she needed. She found she could breathe after all, and her heart settled back into her chest as she settled back into her chair. *The children.* She needed to think of the children and the loss they had suffered. "The children!''

"Calm down. The kids are all alive. Michael even managed to stay conscious long enough to give permission to the hospital to treat them, so there's no worry there. Mickey has a spinal injury. They won't know the full extent of it until they finish tests on him. He's the worst off. Daniel suffered a concussion but he's conscious and seems to be out of danger. Grace has cuts and bruises and is under observation. Rachel was in the rear of the van and wasn't even hurt badly enough to be hospitalized. She's with an emergency care family.''

"Thank you for letting me know in person,'' Maggie said, her voice barely above a whisper. "Who did Sarah and Michael appoint guardians after Trent and I separated? She never said."

Ed grimaced. "Actually, that's why I'm here. They never did change that. You and Trent are still the guardians."

"But Trent and I—"

"Will be divorced by the end of the year. But Sarah never believed it would happen. She said she was praying Trent would change his mind. I tried to convince her but—"

"Sarah is nothing if not stubborn." Maggie felt her stomach bottom out. "Oh…was. She *was*." Maggie bit back tears and pressed her fingertips tightly against her lips. If she started to cry now she might not be able to stop.

"There are going to be a lot of adjustments for you, Maggie."

"But Trent isn't going to change his mind. He doesn't even want any contact with me."

"Maggie, you left *him*."

"And no one regrets that more than I do. I was wrong, but at the time I saw no other way. I guess I was trying to force him to change his mind about an adoption. But he didn't, and I doubt he ever will."

"It isn't all that unusual," Ed said, defending Trent. "He doesn't want to raise someone else's kids. But Michael believed that if something happened to them, Trent would feel differently about raising his own nieces and nephews. And you know as well as I do that Trent agreed to the guardianship without giving it any thought at all. The chance of something happening to both of them was one in a million. And Trent thought Michael led a charmed life, that nothing bad would ever happen to him.''

Maggie just stared at him, still stunned. She and Trent were still their guardians? It was all too much to take in. ''Where is Trent, and how did he take the news?''

''He's in Toronto on business. I called him before I came here. He sounded as if he was in shock at first. He's utterly devastated, Maggie. You know how important Michael was to him. He's flying to Florida as soon as he can get a flight. I don't know when that will be.''

She thought of Sarah and Michael's parents, of their loss. ''Have Nancy and Albertine and Royce Osborne been told?''

Ed's eyes shifted away. ''No. I'll tell them on my way to the airport. I've got us booked on a flight at six. That gives you about an hour-and-a-half to pack a bag and get to the airport.'' Ed stood. ''Meet me at Southern Air's terminal entrance no later than five. Okay?''

Maggie's first glimpse of Trent was at Mickey's bedside the next morning. He was holding his eight-year-old nephew's hand. Trent's face was in profile, his black hair glinted with blue highlights in the sunlight from a nearby window. She stood there just feasting on his face, remembering the wonder and excitement of being held in his arms. Then Mickey's ragged breath drew her attention.

He had tears in his eyes, and, when one fell, Trent

reached up with a tissue to dry it before it ran into the boy's blond hair. "Everything's going to be all right, Mickey," Trent was saying. "The doctors said not being able to feel your legs is normal right now. It doesn't mean anything bad, yet."

Last night when she'd arrived Mickey had been asleep, and it had seemed cruel to wake him with news of his parents' deaths. With Trent not yet there, she had elected to wait to tell Mickey the bad news. Rachel had been another story. She'd been released to a foster family and was apparently inconsolable, having seen her mother dead at the scene and her father and brothers and sister taken off in ambulances.

Ed had remained at the hospital, and Maggie had gone to Rachel. Though the woman taking care of the six-year-old had been kind, she'd also been out of her depth trying to console a grief-stricken child. Maggie had calmed Rachel and reassured her. She'd finally lulled her into an exhausted sleep, but it had been a rough night as nightmares of the crash and its aftermath had haunted the small girl. Maggie had only gotten what little sleep she'd had by lying in the tiny twin bed with her.

This morning Rachel had clung to her, so leaving her behind with a stranger had been impossible. With no clear alternative, Maggie had brought her along to the hospital. Ed was now ensconced with Rachel in a waiting room.

"I want Mommy and Daddy. Where are they?" Mickey demanded.

Maggie let only a tiny sound of distress pass her lips, but Trent twisted in his seat and looked at her.

His startling blue eyes were so filled with pain and confusion that it nearly broke her already shattered heart into even more pieces.

What do I say? those beloved eyes shouted at her.

Praying for the right words, Maggie walked in and stood behind Trent. She put her hand on his shoulder, and he stiffened. Maggie almost removed it, but after a few seconds he seemed to lean into her touch as if he needed her as much as she did him at that moment.

"Mickey," she said.

The child's eyes sought hers. "Aunt Maggie, do you know where Mommy and Daddy are?"

Trent moved closer, dropping to one knee near the head of the bed. His height allowed him the same vantage point he'd had before, and he kept hold of Mickey's hand. Maggie settled into the hard plastic chair Trent had vacated.

"Do you? Do you know where they are?" he asked again.

Maggie nodded, and she saw Trent squeeze Mickey's hand even more tightly. "Do you remember anything about the accident at all?" she asked.

"I woke up from the ambulance noise. Some man was strapping me into a hard bed thing. Rachel was crying and so was Grace."

"A very big truck hit the van while you were sleeping. Everybody but Rachel was hurt. I heard Uncle Trent explaining that you can't feel your legs because your back was injured. Daniel's head is hurt but he's doing fine. Grace was cut by glass and she's doing fine, too. But Mommy and Daddy were in the front of the van where the truck smashed into you. They were both hurt very badly, and the doctors just couldn't help them. Honey, Mommy and Daddy have gone to heaven to be with Jesus.''

Tears filled Mickey's eyes and poured out. His lower lip trembled. "When Pop-Pop Morris went to heaven, I could never see him again. They can't come back to see me either, can they?"

"No honey, but they'll be watching you and you'll always have them right here," she promised, laying her hand over Mickey's heart. "We have to think of what's best for them even though we miss them so very much that it makes us hurt. Because you see, they were both in such terrible pain that Jesus came to take them to heaven where they wouldn't hurt anymore.''

"Do you think that before Jesus came for them they were as scared as I was 'til Uncle Trent came to see me?"

Maggie's eyes met Trent's. "Oh, yes. But hurt and scared as your daddy was, he was more worried about you children. The last thing he did here on earth was to make sure the doctors knew to take care of all of you, and to call us.''

"Aunt Maggie, is it all right for me to be sad? I'm glad Jesus came for them, but I'm still sad.''

"Yes, honey. That's just fine. I'm sad sometimes and miss my daddy. But I know Pop-Pop Morris would never want me to stay sad all the time.''

"I'm still scared, too. Who's going to take care of us now? Who's going to be our mommy and daddy?"

Maggie smiled, hoping to reassure the child, though all she felt was turmoil and conflict. "We will.

Daddy and Mommy made us your guardians. That's a big lawyer word that means Uncle Trent and I will always be here for you.''

Mickey's eyes sought out Trent and his hand came up to pat Trent's cheek. ''Thank you for guarding me, Uncle Trent.'' Mickey's big brown eyes blinked, then closed.

Maggie waited a few moments. ''He's asleep, Trent,'' she whispered. ''Ed wants to talk to both of us.''

Trent let go of Mickey's hand and stood. He looked down at her, his eyes angry. ''That's fine. But we'd better get a few things straight between us first.''

He turned and stalked to the hall. He was hurting, she reminded herself. Trent always processed hurt into anger. She'd never understood why until meeting his parents. They'd never react to something so subtle as hurt feelings. Hurt was something one was expected not to show, to get over alone and then to forget. However cold anger or righteous indignation were acceptable reactions.

Maggie took a deep breath and prayed for guidance, then stood and followed her husband into the hall.

''You did a great job with him,'' Trent said. ''I didn't have a clue how to explain about Mike and Sarah. Thank you.''

''No thanks necessary. I just said what I believe and what Michael and Sarah would have wanted him to hear.''

''You were doing fine until you promised him we'd

both be there for him. You know that isn't the way it's going to be.''

"No. I don't know that. My name is on those guardianship papers, too. And I have no intention of stepping out of their lives when they need me so much. *Any* of their lives. Really, Trent, what do you propose we do? Split them up? You take the boys and I'll take the girls? Increase their loss? Or are you prepared to care for four heartbroken children all by yourself?''

"It isn't you who'll be stepping out of their lives. It'll be me. I've told you. I won't be a father to children who aren't mine. You left me because I wouldn't adopt.''

"And I was wrong. I hurt you and I'm sorry, but this is different. You love them already.''

"But not like a father would.''

"Michael entrusted you with the most precious gift God ever gave him. His children. How can you turn your back on them? Michael's children. These kids are your own flesh and blood.''

Trent flinched. "Maggie, we've been down this route before.''

"But you *love* these kids. I've seen you with them.''

"You've seen an uncle, not a father. I'll never care for them the way a father should. I know that about myself. Just believe me. Finally. Listen to me!''

Maggie stood in a state of complete shock as Trent marched off down the hall. So many thoughts rushed through her head that she had to steady herself by leaning against the wall. Had that been fear she'd just seen in his eyes? Was it that Trent didn't want to *try* loving another person's child, or was he afraid he couldn't? But if that were the case, wouldn't he have explained that to her rather than let his stubborn stand on adoption cause the end of their marriage?

She walked back to the waiting room, still trying to make sense of Trent's anger. The real reason for his anger was usually something other than whatever appeared to be the cause. She tried to step back from the situation and consider what might be going on in his head, but found she was too close to it.

Trent was an adult, though, and would have to deal with his own problems on his own. He'd said often enough in the past three months that he didn't want her in his life. She'd have to take him at his word. The children were all that mattered now. She had just been handed the job of single-handedly supplying security for four helpless lives. And Trent had certainly made it clear that he had no intention of sharing that burden.

Deep in thought, she wove her way through the solarium and stood before the glass wall of windows at the far side. She looked unseeingly up at the heavens, trying to come to terms with all that had happened. Trent's brother was dead. Her best friend Sarah was gone, as well. And their beloved children—their gifts from God, as Sarah and Michael had always called them—were now Maggie's responsibility. Alone.

"Aunt Maggie?"

Maggie turned from the windows and met Rachel's troubled gaze. "Yes, pumpkin?"

"I feel sad. I keep thinking Mommy and Daddy are still here. Then I remember the accident."

"It'll be that way for all of us, for a while but it will get better and those bad memories will fade."

"Mommy looked different after the accident happened. Really different. I think the policeman told me a lie. She didn't look like she was asleep the way he said. Mommy and Daddy aren't asleep, are they? Being in heaven's not like asleep, is it?"

Maggie struggled for the right words, then remembered the service when her father had died and Jim Dillon's explanation of death to the children. Rachel had been a toddler then, so she wouldn't remember. Digging in her purse, Maggie found the peanuts she'd been given on the plane. "See this?" Rachel nodded. "Can you open it?" Rachel took a peanut and studiously opened it. "Now eat it. Chew it all up and swallow it," Maggie instructed, then took the empty peanut shell and fit it back together. "It looks the same but something's different, isn't it? What's different?" she asked.

"It's empty now." Her golden brown eyes were serious.

"That's why Mommy looked so different. Because what you saw was like her shell. What Mommy really was—the really important part of her—was on the inside. Just like the peanut. Where's the peanut now?"

"In my tummy."

"That's right. The peanut is inside you. And so are Mommy and Daddy. All the things they were, and did with you, and all that happiness and love, are tucked right inside of you. And that can make you stronger. Just like the peanut nourishes your body, Mommy and Daddy's memory can nourish your soul. All you have to do is close your eyes and remember a happy time. Let's try it right now. Close your eyes and tell me what you see."

"We had a picnic yesterday with our ice-cream cones. Daddy was sitting down, and Daniel was running around. He tripped and the ice cream came off the cone and fell right on Daddy's head. Daddy looked so surprised and so did Daniel. Then Daddy growled and tackled Daniel and rubbed his gooey hair all over Daniel's shirt, and the cold ice cream got on his tummy. We all just laughed and laughed. Then Mommy acted like they were bad and sent them to the washroom to get clean. It was really funny. Daddy pouted just like Daniel about having to get clean." In a deep voice Rachel said, " 'Do I gotta? Do I gotta?' " Then she giggled. "He was so funny." Her dark eyes flew open, and she hugged Maggie about the hips. "Oh, thank you, Aunt Maggie. I really do feel better."

"I'm glad," Maggie said and hugged Rachel against her. She smoothed a hand over her long strawberry-blond hair, and fought tears.

"Kids are so resilient," Ed said as Rachel skipped off to the play area reserved for children in the corner of the large waiting room.

Maggie narrowed her teary eyes and considered Ed. "Why are you here?" she asked, then added, "Really. No more excuses."

Ed's dry chuckle vibrated in the room. "Always

right to the point, aren't you? Okay. I'm along because I want to make sure your guardianship is clearly established in Florida. It didn't sound as if Mickey will be able to be moved to Pennsylvania any time soon."

"And?" she prodded.

Ed sighed and gestured toward a grouping of sofas and chairs across the room. "Let's sit down. We need to come up with a strategy in case his parents try something. The least I can do is make sure Michael's wishes are carried out. He didn't want those two getting their hands on his kids. He felt so strongly about it that he made me write it in his will."

"How did his parents take the news of their deaths?" Maggie asked as she settled across from Ed.

"About the way you'd expect. They looked shocked at first, then 'appropriately' sad for a few seconds each. Next came the legal questions and annoyance that you and Trent were named guardians."

"Sounds just like my loving parents," Trent said from behind them. "What else did they say?" he asked as he walked to stand in front of them.

"That, in light of your separation, of course they would be happy to 'take the kids off your hands,' Trent."

Anger flared in Maggie's gaze. "Take them off Trent's hands! I guess they knew their oldest son at least. He *doesn't* want them. He just told me. And what did they say about me?"

"As far as they're concerned, you don't enter the equation. The children aren't your blood relatives, so the Osbornes feel you have no rights regardless of their son's will." Ed fixed Trent with a steely look. "We're in for trouble if you keep this up, Trent, because your parents will never let Maggie raise those kids alone. Not only should you not continue with the divorce, but I suggest you consider moving into Michael and Sarah's house. Together."

Chapter Two

Trent's heart thundered, echoing in his head. *None of this is happening,* his mind screamed. But there was no waking from this living nightmare. Maggie stared up at him, pushing her dark chestnut hair behind her ear, her deep brown eyes wide and expectant. It hurt just being in the room with her, knowing he couldn't even reach out and touch her, yet wanting—no, needing to. And to have her look at him with so much hope and anxiety nearly destroyed his control.

He turned away.

And his gaze came to rest on little Rachel across the room in a play center, rocking the tattered baby doll that had been her constant companion since her first birthday. There she sat, a sweet child, loving that doll as if it were still clean and pretty, fresh from the box. He blinked away sudden burning in his eyes. His parents would destroy that sweetness and throw that "disgraceful thing" in the trash. He knew because he remembered his own fury when one day just after he'd started school his own blue bear had disappeared.

And Mickey. If he didn't improve, they'd see him as "damaged." Trent would never forget overhearing his mother railing at Michael's fourth-grade teacher for suggesting that he was learning disabled. "My son is not damaged! You are just an inferior teacher," she'd told the woman. And poor Michael had stood there with her, hearing it all and knowing that his teacher was right: he didn't learn the way the others did. And so he began to view himself as damaged. The trouble started just after that fateful day.

No. His parents wouldn't be good for these kids. They would destroy them one day—one subtle cruelty at a time. Even *he* would be better because he understood the damage idle words could cause. And he'd watch everything he said around the children. He would never let down his guard. He knew he'd never find it in himself to be a real father to them, but he would make sure he was never cruel.

So it's decided, then. He and Maggie would become their guardians together. He turned back into the room. Doubt assailed him once again. How would he deal with Maggie? He'd loved her so deeply, and yet he'd been unable to give her what she wanted most. Children. And so she'd left him. Telling him without words that a long-dead dream was more important than their love for each other.

But now she'll have both, a traitorous voice whispered. *And you can have her back.* He suddenly ached to be able to forget his current anguish, in her arms.

But the day she'd left with tears in her eyes, he'd sworn never to let her return. Never again to open his heart to that kind of pain. And never to inflict it on Maggie, either.

Because, as hurt as he had been by her decision, he'd known she suffered as well. He'd lived with that pain for years, knowing all the while that it was his fault, that he was keeping her from fulfilling her dreams of having children.

He'd grown up knowing his parents didn't love him. And it had been fear during those years that had held him back. Fear that, never having received love as a boy, he would not know how to give love to a child. And he'd been right to be afraid, because now he found he had no idea how to be a loving parent.

Trent knew not only how an unloved child felt, but the pain of knowing he'd been adopted and that his real parents hadn't wanted him, either. He'd also been burdened by the knowledge that his parents didn't even see him as a part of their family. It was a shame he'd carried nearly his whole life.

He'd been about to enter junior high when he'd come downstairs late one night to raid the refrigerator. He'd heard his parents discussing sending him away to boarding school...

"I just keep looking at Trenton, wondering what to do with him, Royce."

"There's only one answer. Ruxley is an excellent school."

"It seems so unfair, sending him and not Michael.

But I can't let Michael go away. There is simply no way I will."

"Still, that's no reason to keep Trenton here," his father said. "The instructors there will know what to do with a boy like him to bring out all his potential."

"And who knows what his potential is? His mother and father couldn't have been Rhodes scholars considering their poor backgrounds."

"Albertine, it's too soon to see if heredity or environment will tell with him."

His mother laughed bitterly. "You don't need to remind me. Michael is our biological child, and he's already nothing like either of us."

"Have you given any more thought to having another child?"

"I spoke with Mother. She believes that only animals have more than two children. She said that even if we were willing to let people know Trenton is adopted, another child would still be out of the question. She's always thought we were foolish to adopt him, and now she's gloating." His mother sighed. "So even though medically having another child is now an option, I've decided to just devote my time to Michael."

"It's your decision, of course," his father said, but he sounded annoyed.

His mother typically ignored the censure in her husband's tone. "Yes, it is. I'll, of course, leave the decision about Trenton to your discretion. If you want to send him away to Ruxley, then I have no objections, but I won't hear of it for Michael. It may actually be better for him if we do send Trenton to boarding school.''

''I understand your feelings about Michael. I'll tell Trenton in the morning.''

''Fine. And Royce, try to present this as an exciting opportunity and not punishment and exile....''

Trent hadn't waited to hear more. When his father called him to his study the next day, Trent hadn't let on that he knew Ruxley was indeed punishment and exile, and not the honor they claimed. And he'd never let them know that he knew about his adoption, fearing that they would then reject him altogether and he would lose Mike from his life as well.

That overheard conversation had been a defining moment in Trent's life. He'd understood at last why they treated him so differently from his brother. Cold as they were to Mike at times, they'd never sent him away. They'd been there to get him out of scrape after scrape. Of course, Michael had characterized their attention as so intense it was smothering. But at least it had been attention.

They certainly hadn't smothered Trent. In fact, they hadn't even bothered to come to his high school, college or graduate school graduations. The day he'd stood addressing his fellow students as Stanford's valedictorian with no family in the audience, he'd silently vowed that he would never have children. He knew that people usually treat their own children the way they've been treated, and he feared he'd do just that.

Then he'd met Maggie. And had fallen head over

heels in love with her. He'd loved her so much that he'd fooled himself into believing he'd be able to love a child of that love as much as he did her. But Maggie had been busy establishing her career, and so they'd decided to wait for their first child. For five years Maggie had looked forward to the day when she'd made enough of a name for herself as an interior designer that she could cut her hours and work from home, caring for their baby. The delay, however, had given Trent's doubts long enough to creep in, and deep inside he'd become afraid again that he wouldn't know how to love a child. To his shame, he'd been relieved when Maggie had been unable to conceive even with the help of fertility experts. Everything had been working out just fine.

Then she'd brought up the idea of adoption, and panic had overwhelmed him. He had known he'd fail an innocent child as his parents had failed him. He'd told her no—he didn't believe in adoption. He would not adopt and raise someone else's child. Though he hadn't failed some unknown child, he *had* ultimately failed Maggie and himself. And all because he hadn't been able to open his heart to her about the real reason for his stand: his shame of being so unlovable to both sets of his parents that no one had loved him as a child. No one had shown him how to love children.

And he'd stood just as firm about reconciliation. Better not to hurt each other again and again over needs and shortcomings neither could change. He'd gone against his every instinct and need by pushing Maggie away when she'd changed her mind about trying again to make their marriage work.

But now there was this—this unbearable tragedy. Mike and Sarah were really gone. He'd just come from viewing their bodies. And now, apparently, his parents wanted the children. Another tragedy in the making.

Trent looked up, his decision suddenly made. He saw Ed looking at him expectantly. "Stop the divorce," he said. "We'll put it back together. Maggie and the kids can move into that Victorian monstrosity Sarah talked Mike into, if that's what you think would look best. But don't expect me to—"

"Hold it right there, Trent," Ed interrupted. "I'll get right on halting the divorce action, but I shouldn't hear about anything less than complete reconciliation. I need to have a clear conscience if we have to go head-to-head with your parents in court. And in that case, you'd better have a complete family unit to present to the judge. Your parents aren't so advanced in years that a judge wouldn't hand those kids over to them if he thought you and Maggie were providing an unhealthy home environment. Take my word for it, living in an armed camp would be construed as unhealthy."

Trent pursed his lips and nodded, knowing Ed walked a fine line being both his counsel and friend. "I was only going to say not to expect me to be home every night. I'll have to keep the apartment in the city. Late-night meetings and long drives home aren't a good combination, especially if you add long workdays and icy streets in the winter."

"You two can work out the details, but I'd advise you to think about cutting those long hours at least a little. And Maggie, what do you intend to do about your job? Have you thought about it at all?''

''I enjoy my work and the challenge it presents, but I think four children under the age of nine will be challenge enough for some time to come, don't you?''

Trent couldn't believe his ears. Maggie loved her job. Even when they'd been trying to have a child of their own, she'd never intended to give up her career completely. ''But you worked so hard to get where you are,'' he said, not understanding how she could have reached her apparent decision so quickly. ''I can't let you give all that up. You need to think this through. We'll hire someone to help with the children. Mike and I had a nanny until I went away to school.''

''I'm not averse to hiring someone to help with housework and cooking, but not a nanny. You and your brother hadn't lost your parents, and considering the ones you had, a nanny was probably the best thing to ever happen to you. These children have lost the most important people in their lives, and they're going to need all the love and attention they can get for a good long time. I intend to be there to give it to them. It's a done deal, Trent. I already resigned before I left the office yesterday.''

Trent stiffened. Why didn't she seem upset by the sacrifice of a career that had taken over a decade to build? *Because it isn't a sacrifice! He'd lost his brother, but she had just been handed everything she'd always wanted on a silver platter.* ''A house in the country. Children. And me. This is just perfect for you, isn't it?" he sneered. "A real win-win situation."

"Trent!" Ed gasped.

Trent lost control of all he'd felt in the past twenty-four hours. Deaf to the outrage in his friend's voice and blind to the horror written on Maggie's lovely features, he let it all boil forth—the pain, the anguish, the confusion. "You were awfully sure of what my decision would be regarding Mike's kids. Suppose I'd decided to take them myself and hire a nanny."

Pale and shaken, Maggie squared her shoulders. "I wasn't at all sure what you'd decide to do. I was only sure that *I'd* do what Sarah and Michael wanted me to do—which was be a mother to their children. Nothing and no one is going to stop me from fulfilling that promise. Not even you. And for the record, both Sarah and Michael were a very important part of my life. I grew up with Sarah as a sister. They were the only friends who stood by me these last months. I've lost, too, Trent. You aren't the only one grieving."

Ed stood, his anger obvious. "I think I'll go keep Rachel company. Distract her. Work this out between you. I won't be surprised if Royce and Albertine sail in here any minute now, so you probably don't have a lot of time. Trent, you have to find a way to put the past aside and look toward the future. This kind of atmosphere will destroy those kids. And your parents aren't stupid. They'll spot any lingering animosity from a mile away and then figure out a way to prove it's there to a judge. Talk this out…and fast."

Trent suddenly felt as if the weight of the world were pressing down on his shoulders. He sank into the chair Ed had vacated next to Maggie. Elbows on his knees he stared at his hands. He couldn't even believe he'd thought those things of Maggie, let alone said them. Overwhelmed by the magnitude of all that had happened, his eyes filled. "I'm sorry. That was uncalled for."

"And I'm sorry for all that's happened," she whispered. Maggie moved to sit in front of him on a small glass coffee table. She took his hands between hers. He closed his eyes, absorbing the feelings her touch evoked—the comfort, the closeness, the need. He didn't feel so alone now. "I know how much you loved Michael," she went on. "And Sarah. And I know it's terribly hard to deal with *us* on top of your grief. But we have to. We're the adults in this situation, and those kids are counting on us. Michael and Sarah are, too."

Trent nodded. "I know. It's just so hard to even think clearly right now. I really didn't mean what I said."

"It's true that I've prayed and prayed for the Lord to find a way to bring us back together. I told you that just last week, so I can't deny it. But not like this, Trent. Never like this. Believe me, if living alone on some mountaintop for the rest of my life and never seeing you again would bring those two strolling through that door over there, I'd have started packing yesterday. But life just doesn't always come with room for bargaining."

Deeply ashamed of his outburst, Trent nodded. "I truly didn't mean it. Any of it. You know that, don't you? I don't even know why I said it." He looked up into Maggie's sad smile.

"You said it because you're hurting. You only get angry when you're hurting," she told him and squeezed his hands. He could almost have sworn he felt strength flow from her to him. "Try to think of them happy in heaven. It'll help."

Trent blinked, startled. "You really believe that?"

"Oh, yes." She smiled again in that sad, sort of wistful way, but it was a smile nonetheless. Where did her strength come from?

Could it be from God? "It's what Mike believed, I know." Trent stared at their hands but his thoughts were of Mike. He'd gotten deeply into religion and his church. He'd always been a little weak—religion was sort of a crutch, after all. It had changed Mike for the better, though. There was no denying that. What this Jesus thing had done for his little brother was nothing short of a miracle, but Trent didn't need a miracle. He was intelligent, responsible and a success in the business world. But then, so was Maggie. So how had she gotten sucked into that church of theirs?

"Maybe we don't have to deal with our situation right now, after all," Maggie suggested. "For now, let's just deal with the logistics of the changes we need to make in our lives, and take care of what the kids need."

Not him for a father, that was for sure, Trent thought. "Maggie, I won't be a father to those kids. I'm their uncle and I love them like an uncle. I'll support them financially. I'll be to them what I always have been, but I won't try to be their father. I'll come to the house at night when I can. Spend Saturdays doing the suburban home-owner routine when I'm not away on business. But that's it. Don't ask for more. Because more just isn't in me.''

Maggie took his face between her hands. ''You just be the best uncle you know how to be, and it'll be better than most kids get in a father. I know it'll be better than what you and Michael had. That's for sure. And I promise to be here to help any way you need me.''

Trent stared into her eyes, humbled as always. Maggie had always had a bottomless well of confidence in him. In fact, she'd left him because he'd refused to try to live up to her expectations. He hoped she was right. He hoped he could give the kids enough as their uncle. Because he was trapped. And as always, Mike was counting on him.

Grief, stunning and overwhelming, suddenly crashed in on him, crushing him. Maggie's form blurred as tears filled his eyes. Trent instinctively blinked them back, but something drove him to reach for Maggie, pulling her into his arms. In his grief, he forgot every need having her close would normally elicit. His throat ached. ''How can this be happening? How? He always landed on his feet. Why not this time?''

''Really, Trenton,'' a female voice interrupted. ''Get hold of yourself. You're making a public spectacle. I thought at least we'd taught you better about that.''

Maggie stiffened, and Trent opened his eyes to

stare over her shoulder at the couple in the doorway. So, they'd arrived, just as Ed had thought they would. Both dressed in gray, they looked as impeccable as always. And rigid. And haughty. Not exactly the ideal attributes in parents or grandparents. Rachel's chatter to Ed stopped, and Trent spit out an oath as he set Maggie away and stood.

"Actually, Mother, showing honest emotions like grief is not generally considered a spectacle these days, and as you can see we have the room to ourselves. We were all family here," he added pointedly.

"Other than your mother and me, the only family members here are you and the girl," his father said. "We need to talk without outsiders present."

Maggie stood as if to leave, but Trent wrapped his arm around her waist. "Maggie is my wife, Father. She *is* family. *My* family. And Ed stays because we have nothing to say to either of you unless our lawyer is present."

"Trenton, that is hardly necessary. After all, we are all interested in what is best for the children," his mother countered.

"That's why I don't intend to allow either of you to have any say whatsoever in their futures. That's what Mike specified in his will, and I intend to see his and Sarah's wishes are carried out."

Royce Osborne's cold gray eyes bored into him, but Trent refused to let him see how much he wished their relationship could be different. He supposed children never stopped wanting their parents' approval, even years after they stopped trying to win it.

"You can't hope to win against us in court," Royce said.

"Why? Ed's a top-notch attorney. And he wrote an ironclad will."

"Because you and your wife are about to be divorced. What do you intend to do with the children? Raise them alone? Our lawyer assures us that no court in the land will give those children to a single man with a demanding career."

Trent frowned. "Alone? Where did you get the idea that I'd even consider raising the children without my wife? Maggie's already handed in her resignation so she can be with them full time."

"You're about to be divorced! Do you intend to split custody? You can't really believe the court will side with you and allow that?" Royce sneered.

"Actually the divorce is old news. Maggie and I have been talking about a reconciliation for a while, now." Trent felt Maggie stiffen. It wasn't really a lie. They *had* been talking about it for weeks. He'd rejected the idea time and again, but his parents didn't need to know that.

"I knew she came to see you last week, but from what I hea—" His mother cut herself off midword.

And where would she hear anything about us? Trent wondered. He'd have asked, but as the thought occurred to him Maggie gave a subtle nod toward the other side of the room. Rachel was staring from the play center at them. "I really have no more to say on the subject," he said at once, seeing Rachel detach herself from Ed and start toward them.

"Uncle Trent!" Rachel called as she ran across the

room. "Cindy had a nightmare." She climbed up on the chair next to him and handed him Cindy, the well-loved baby doll.

His mother gasped and recoiled. "Good heavens I'm surprised the nurses didn't burn that filthy thing!"

Rachel clamped herself to his waist, and Trent defiantly took the doll and put it on his shoulder, giving it a pat and kiss. Rachel beamed up at him, her big brown eyes alight with gratitude, and took back her lifelong treasure with a huge hug. Without sparing her grandparents more than a glance, Rachel went back to Ed, selecting yet another book on the way.

"She's completely undisciplined and rude!" his mother gasped.

"Albertine, shouldn't you be grateful that Rachel has settled down so well?" Maggie asked quietly. "The accident was very traumatic for her, and she spent all of last night in a very bad state."

"There is no excuse for rudeness. She interrupted adults in the middle of a conversation. I can see you'd be no better at parenting those children than Michael and his wife were. That is precisely why I want a hand in raising our grandchildren."

Trent had had enough. He pitched his voice low so he'd be sure Rachel couldn't hear. "That child saw her mother's dead body pulled from that wreckage. This morning Maggie had to tell her Mike had died as well. I'd think that's all the excuse she needs to be a little rude. For crying out loud, Mother, she's six-and-a-half years old!" He paused, wondering if anything he'd said had cracked their icy control. It hadn't. His parents just stared at him blankly. "Your son is dead," he tried again. "Can't you even show emotion over that? Don't you care?"

Royce narrowed his eyes. "Of course we care but Michael had all but cut us out of his life since his marriage. I don't know why it surprised us. He never lived up to his potential. He became an auto mechanic, for pity's sake. We barely saw him these past years. What did you expect us to feel?"

Trent felt ready to explode, but Maggie's hand moved over his back—soothing, comforting. "Nothing. I don't expect you to feel anything. You never have. Why should this be any different? I think you should leave. You don't belong here," he told them.

"Trenton—" his mother began.

"*Now*, Mother." Trent's voice was steely. "Or I'm going to make a scene the likes of which will visit you in your nightmares for years."

"We came to see the children," Royce demanded.

"The children are awfully fragile right now, Royce," Maggie warned.

"Maggie's right," Trent added. "They are fragile. Too fragile to deal with virtual strangers. Please, just go back home. No good will come from your being here. Someone will let you know what the funeral arrangements are."

"Since I'm certain they'll have something to do with those fanatics who meet in that converted barn, we'll just see you in court," his father said. Nearly identical frowns in place, they turned as one and left.

Ed approached from the other end of the large

room. "Not a pretty sight," he murmured. "Did that go as badly as it looked?"

Trent sighed. "They won't be at the funeral, and they'll see us in court."

Chapter Three

During the ten years of her marriage, Maggie had been in the company of her in-laws only a handful of times. She knew them to be stiff, formal people. She'd felt uncomfortable with them even though they hadn't objected to her marriage to Trent. They'd hosted the usual engagement party and rehearsal dinner, and Albertine had attended her bridal shower. But when Michael had fallen head over heels for her maid of honor, Maggie had seen their true colors—the people behind the polite facades they presented to the world. It had been an eye-opener, not a very pretty sight.

Sarah was the daughter of Maggie's mother's live-in maid. She and Sarah had grown up together. When Maggie had been headed for an exclusive private high school, her father had pulled some strings, donated some money to the school and arranged for Sarah to attend on a scholarship. There wasn't a day of Mag-

gie's life when Sarah hadn't been there—'til now—
and back then, they'd been inseparable.

At first, any friend of Maggie's was good enough
for Michael, as far as her in-laws had been concerned.
But then Sarah had made the grave error of explaining
their lifelong friendship. The Osbornes' opinion had
changed in the blink of an eye on learning that Sarah
was the child of a maid.

But Michael had loved Sarah to distraction. He'd
agreed to begin attending services with her on Sundays. The change in him had been dramatic, but Maggie hadn't understood the source of that change back
then. She'd thought her friend Sarah was solely responsible. But she'd been wrong. Jesus, working in
the life of a misunderstood, angry young man, had
sparked the changes.

But whatever the source, Trent had been thrilled
when wild, unpredictable Michael had stopped getting
into scrapes with the local police that Trent or their
parents had to pay his way out of. After a few weeks,
Michael had gone to Trent and told him that he
wanted to go to school to learn to be an auto mechanic. Trent finally seeing real excitement in his
brother's eyes about learning something, had loaned
him the money without a thought. And for the first
time in his life Michael had flourished.

A year later, Michael and Sarah had been married
at Maggie's parents' home, under the same rose trellis
where Maggie and Trent had stood a year earlier. Michael had invited his parents even though they didn't
approve of Sarah's background. And they had attended. But it had been painfully obvious that they'd

only gone because they hadn't wanted their friends to know that Michael's choice of a bride was causing a rift in the family. But there *was* a rift. And only now, hearing her in-laws denigrate Michael even in death, did Maggie realize how deep it had gone.

"I'm sorry, Trent," Ed said with a grimace. "This is one of those times I wish I'd been wrong, but I had a feeling they'd pull something like this."

Trent grimaced and shook his head. "No. It's better this way. Now that the other shoe has dropped, we know for sure where it is."

Maggie dropped her arm from Trent's waist. "I'm stunned. They've always been hard people, and you and Michael haven't been close to them since before he and Sarah married. But to belittle Michael that way, and in front of one of his children, is unbelievable."

"And unforgivable. The worst part of the whole thing is that they don't care about the kids. It's the appearance that they do that matters to them. And they probably just don't want *me* raising them." Trent looked uncomfortable, as if he'd revealed something accidentally.

"It's probably more that they don't want me involved," Maggie said. "She's always held my acceptance of Sarah as an equal against me. And did you hear that crack about our church? The one about me being as bad as Sarah at raising them was a little strange, though. How would she know what kind of mother Sarah was? This whole thing is just so unbelievable. If Albertine was always scandalized by the number of children they had, why would she want to raise them? That letter she wrote to Sarah when she heard Grace was on the way was nothing short of cruel. 'Only animals have more than two children'? When Sarah called and read it to me, she was in tears and Michael was furious.''

Trent frowned but remained silent. Trent had been even angrier with his parents than Michael had. Maggie had wondered why then, and wondered again now, noticing his eyes glitter with suppressed fury.

"I'll keep an eye out for it in case they saved it," Maggie promised, hoping to change the subject.

Ed's smile was almost mischievous. "They did, and now I have it. Michael was smarter than most people gave him credit for. He was determined that if something happened to him, Sarah would have plenty of ammunition in case his parents went after custody. And he was sure they would. They blamed Sarah for every step Michael took in a direction that they didn't approve of."

"Speaking of the children," Maggie said. "I think we should go check on them. I haven't seen Grace or Daniel yet today, and they were asleep when I saw them yesterday. I wonder if the hospital would let Rachel in to see them. I think it would do all of them a world of good to be together. Especially Mickey."

Trent and Ed needed to sign papers for the release and transportation of Mike's and Sarah's bodies back to Pennsylvania, so Maggie took Rachel along with her to see the others. The nurses in pediatrics, who had shuffled patients to put Mickey's siblings in the room next to him, saw no problem with one more child visiting.

Rachel went immediately to Daniel, who was alone in a crib on the left near the windows. Maggie walked to the other crib where Grace slept on her side, facing into the room, her teddy bear clutched in a death grip. The bandage on Grace's upper-left arm covered a laceration that would no doubt leave a nasty scar, as would the one on her thigh that had been caused by the flying glass. Amazingly, she hadn't suffered facial injuries. Maggie looked into her little cherub face and touched her carrot-red curls. Careful not to wake her, Maggie then tiptoed away to Daniel. She could hear grumbling across the room about having been put in a crib like a baby.

And then the hard part began.

"Where are Mommy and Daddy?" he asked.

It had been a long day, Maggie thought at almost midnight, as she tossed the last little outfit into the laundry bag and leaned against the wall. Grace was too young to understand that Mommy and Daddy were in heaven and wouldn't be back. She'd just wanted her parents, but Maggie's familiar face had gone a long way toward soothing her and making her feel more secure. Daniel understood a little more and oddly had been more easily consoled. He was nowhere near as aware of the changes ahead as Mickey and Rachel, though.

It was Mickey who worried Maggie the most—and not just because of his medical condition. He was too quiet. Too detached from all that was happening. After a conference with his doctor, Maggie and Trent had decided she would have to remain in Florida with the other children until Mickey could safely be moved to a hospital back home.

By the end of the day, Trent and Ed somehow had found and rented a small furnished house not far from the hospital. Ed had taken Maggie to rent a van which they'd equipped with a car seat for Grace, while Trent had visited with the children.

He was so good with them—teasing smiles out of Grace, reading stories to Rachel and Daniel, and playing board games with Mickey—that Maggie was confused. Why was Trent so sure that he would be a poor father? It simply made no sense.

But whether he was ready for parenthood or not, the children, except for Mickey, had been ready to be released by the end of the day. Grace was badly bruised in addition to the lacerations, and she was cranky and out of sorts. Plus, Maggie was sure Grace felt the tension of the adults who populated her world and was reacting to it.

Grace had finally drifted off about an hour ago, after Maggie spent time rocking her. Trent, meanwhile, had read several stories to Rachel and Daniel, had supplied the requisite extra glass of water and had tucked them in—several times.

And so now it was midnight and all the children were finally settled. Maggie pushed away from the wall, knowing she had one more task to perform. She had to talk to Trent and get him to talk to her. She found him in the living room, staring out the patio doors at the rain.

"I hope this weather doesn't mean you'll have a

rough flight in the morning. What time do you take off?''

Trent glanced back at her for a second. ''Not until ten. The first available flight was at dawn, but I didn't think it would be good for the kids to have another adult just disappear on them.''

Maggie stared at him. Even she hadn't thought of that. Trent became more of a puzzle about the children every time he opened his mouth. ''Are you too tired to talk awhile?'' she asked. ''I thought we should formalize some plans.''

Trent turned, his smile bitter. ''We've been married ten years, Mag. Why not say what you mean? You've never had trouble expressing your feelings in the past. I seem to remember several dissertations on my faults that lasted a good long while before you walked out.''

''Fine. Where do we stand?'' she asked flatly.

Trent visibly started. ''I—I don't know.''

Maggie closed her eyes and took a deep breath. *Please help me say the right things, Lord.* ''I shouldn't have left you, Trent. Both Michael and Sarah tried to tell me that I still loved you too much to start over without you, but I wouldn't listen. I couldn't see past the emptiness inside me that called out for a child. Then I left and the emptiness grew. I managed to achieve so many of the goals I thought I wanted—the house in Valley Forge, the reduced hours at work. I found that hole I'd wanted to fill with a child filled with the love of Jesus. Then I found out that even as a single parent I had a chance for a foreign adoption, but the emptiness only got worse because you weren't there to share it with me.''

Maggie blinked to clear her swimming vision. "I was wrong. I promised you for better or worse, but when worse came along, I folded my tent and walked off. I can't change what I did. I can only tell you how sorry I am and will be for the rest of my life. I can only tell you that I love you. And that I'd like to try to make it all up to you."

Trent closed his eyes and sighed. "I don't honestly see how you can."

Maggie felt the pain of his words in every pore of her body, but she prayed for strength and found it. She reached out and laid her hand on his arm. He stiffened at her touch and tears flooded her eyes, overflowing down her cheek, blurring her focus. "Please let me try. Please."

Narrowing his blue eyes, he stared at her for a long moment. "I don't know." He turned and walked away, dropping into the rattan sofa against the far wall of the small parlor. He was silent for several minutes, staring ahead. Then he looked back over at her. In his eyes she saw such stark longing and desire that she gasped, but his clenched teeth and hand said that his need for her still warred with pain and anger. "Why don't you tell me why I should?" he demanded.

"Because I've never stopped loving you. And I think it's God's plan that we be together."

"You left me!" he shouted, his voice breaking, his anguish bursting through the anger.

And that pain—pain she'd inflicted—felt like a knife in her heart. "I know it won't be easy for either of us, but I think we can salvage our marriage."

"It was you who decided to scuttle our marriage in the first place."

Regret had never weighed more heavily on Maggie's shoulders. She walked to the sofa and sat on an ottoman placed nearby. The hurt and confusion on his face nearly overwhelmed her. How could she have done this to him? "I'm sorry I left you. I'm sorry for all the arguments before I did. But we have ten years together behind us, and the raising of four children ahead of us. I think those are fourteen pretty good reasons to try again. And you can't say I only want to try now because of the children. You know I felt this way before the accident. Even before I learned about the foreign adoption possibilities. You know that!"

"And I told you how I felt every time you contacted me."

Had he decided not to reconcile, after all? She braced herself. "This morning you told Ed you were agreeable to getting back together. Have you changed your mind?"

Trent shook his head. "The kids need both of us to protect them from my parents. I just don't know how to handle you and me."

"You could try relying on the Lord. It's the best way I've found to face adversity."

"I don't even know what that means. Who is this Lord? A God who cares about us? Who fixes things and changes lives? I sure never met Him at the church I grew up in. He's a concept I can't even relate to."

Maggie nodded. The last she'd heard from Michael, Trent still saw faith as a crutch. At least now he was questioning in his own way. "How about taking it one day at a time? How about looking at me and the kids as a package deal. Please say you'll move into the house with us. That you'll be waiting for us when we come back north."

"I...I'm not sure. I just don't know if I can. I'm going to *have* to play it by ear. Like you said. One day at a time."

Trent stared at the key in his hand. Then at the lock. He'd waited a week since the memorial service and funeral. And he knew he couldn't put it off any longer. The last time he'd talked to Mike, his brother had most of the house torn apart to put in a new climate-control plant. Which meant there was not only no heat or air-conditioning, but no hot water, either. Ed had called to warn Trent that if his parents did sue for custody, a home study would be done on both environments.

One step at a time, he reminded himself, and turned the key. But when he went inside, he wished he could take back that last step. He hadn't understood: this wasn't torn apart—it had been demolished. There were almost no walls! What had they been thinking to call this mess a paradise. It sure didn't look like *Paradise Found* to him! It was more like *Paradise Lost!*

Trent closed his eyes, then slowly opened them again. Nothing had changed. Studs. Subflooring. Exposed pipes. Then he remembered the kitchen Mike had mentioned finishing. A bathroom and a room he'd created as a family room from two smaller ones at the back of the house. Mike had begun the project shortly after Maggie walked out on their marriage. How could nearly nine months have gone by since he visited Mike and Sarah at their own house?

He'd seen them often, but at his place. He'd met them at the zoo one day. Had taken them to a lake in Jersey another. But he hadn't come to their home. Mike had told him the place was torn up, and Trent had used it as an excuse because he was afraid to run into Maggie. Afraid he'd weaken, take her back. Afraid he'd pull her into his arms, kiss her senseless and beg her to forgive him for denying her the children she needed, then never let her go.

Trent shook his head and picked his way through the entrance foyer, past the remnants of a sweeping staircase, and down the hall to the kitchen for which Mike had been so full of plans. He pushed open the leaded-glass swinging door, and stood spellbound.

The room stood like a monument to his brother's talent. For so long Mike had been told that to work with his hands would be unseemly. Trent didn't know Mike's Lord, but he thanked Him just the same, because somehow He'd given his brother the courage to be who he was meant to be. And now Trent understood why Mike and Sarah had named the house Paradise Found.

Black granite counters gleamed. Oak cabinets shone. It was…overwhelming in its beauty. He ran his hands over the cabinets and the frosted leaded-glass inserts. He recognized the cabinet doors that framed the glass. On his last visit, just after a particularly nasty fight with Maggie, Mike had shown Trent the prototype he'd just finished. Sarah's art—bordered by Mike's.

Tears flooded his eyes. Trent made his way to the kitchen table and dropped his head onto his forearm where it rested on the table. Some minutes later he found himself stroking the surface of the big round oak table. Lifting his head he noticed that it sat in a large alcove with tall windows affording a wonderful view of the woods that bordered the back lawn. Wainscoting, painted taupe, came up to the sill of the windows, and Victorian print paper graced the small amount of wall space left by the windows.

Trent looked back at the surface of the table. He ran his hand over it again, marveling at the smoothness of the hand-rubbed patina. His brother again. Trent had seen it months ago, in pieces and stripped to its nicked surface in Mike's workshop.

He looked out the window and realized that his brother had created the alcove by bumping the walls out into the back porch. Curious, he went to the door and out onto the porch. The porch hadn't suffered, but now followed the four walls of the interior alcove. The bump-out caused the porch roof to form a mini turret. Like most of the house, the porch wasn't finished. But Trent could visualize exactly what Mike had planned.

And plans reminded him of Mike's workshop in the old carriage house. He jumped down off the unfinished back porch and headed that way, but he hesitated once he reached the threshold, not sure he could take many more haunting memories. Trent looked back at the house and the new, unpainted wood of the porch. Resolutely he turned and unlocked the workshop door.

The memories came at once. Painful, poignant and wonderful, they flooded in. The odor of newly planed wood. The smell of Sarah's soldering gun. Mike, his safety glasses perched on his head, grinning over the floor plans. Sarah, tossing a wad of paper at Mike in retaliation for his incessant teasing, her sweet loving smile shining in her eyes.

He glanced at those same sparkling eyes in the picture on one of the shelves above Mike's workbench. It was a candid shot of the four of them that had been taken on Mike and Sarah's wedding day. A day that had almost not happened, thanks to his parents.

They'd been horrified when Sarah had innocently revealed that she wasn't Maggie's neighbor but that they'd lived on the same property—Maggie in the main house and Sarah as the daughter of the maid in the apartment over the carriage house. Seeing Sarah as a lower-class influence on Michael, they'd tried to pay her to get out of Michael's life.

Trent would never forget the day he'd opened his door to find Sarah, pale and shaking like a leaf in a hurricane, the check still clutched convulsively in her hand. Trent had shouted for Maggie immediately and had called Mike to come to their apartment. And nothing had been the same between either the two sons and their parents since.

Mike had moved in with him and Maggie for a while, and later Trent had become Mike's silent partner in an auto garage that catered to luxury cars and their owners. It had been a great joke between him and his brother that growing up with parents like theirs had ensured the business's success by teaching Mike exactly how to deal with the finicky demands of many of the Main-Line's wealthy residents.

Trent shook his head as he stared at those four smiling faces. They all looked so happy—and they had been. But now everything was different. It was hard to think of them as gone. The workshop *felt* as if they were still there.

And so did the house, he realized, and glanced at the slot next to the picture. The floor plans Mike had drawn up were where he'd always kept them. Pulling them out of the cubbyhole, Trent watched his hand shake. He unrolled them and found more there than just the blueprints he'd seen before. Every idea and plan Mike and Sarah had decided on was cataloged. Wallpaper swatches, paint colors, quantities needed and estimated costs—all were there.

An hour later the house had taken shape in Trent's mind.

The monstrosity no longer seemed that, he realized, but another page in the unfinished book that his brother's life had become when an overtired trucker had driven on into the night instead of pulling over. And like the raising of Mike's kids, it was another thing Trent knew he would see through to its finish. He owed that to Mike, the one person who had loved him unconditionally.

With that thought, another devastating one occurred to him. ''Maybe I should have given him a chance. Maybe if I'd told him I wasn't really his brother, he would have loved me anyway," Trent said aloud. "Maybe he still would have *wanted* to be my brother."

Chapter Four

"Aunt Maggie," Rachel said, "are we really going to leave Mickey here? Why can't he come home with us?"

Maggie glanced at Rachel in the rearview mirror of the rental van she'd picked up at the airport. "Mickey's going to be fine at Shriners. You saw all the other kids. He'll have lots of company and get the therapy he needs. We can come visit, and before you know it, he'll be home with us, driving you crazy the way he used to."

"I love you, Aunt Maggie, but I wish it could be like it used to be. I even prayed for it a few times, but I know it can't happen."

You aren't the only one praying for the impossible, Maggie thought. "I love you, too, sweetheart, and I understand how you feel."

Two weeks had settled the two younger children into a secure routine with her, but Rachel and Mickey were having a tougher time adjusting. Rachel, at least, talked about her grief and loss. Not so Mickey. He was still silent and deeply depressed.

"Will Uncle Trent be at our house?" Rachel asked from behind her.

"That's what I'm thinking," she said, and forced what she hoped was a confident-looking smile. In truth, she had no clue where Trent was. She'd been unable to reach him to tell him they were returning. She'd left message after message on his answering machine at home and on his voice mail at work but he hadn't gotten in touch with her. By late yesterday she'd swallowed her pride and called his secretary's extension. Ellen told her that he'd taken a few days off, that her orders were not to disturb him unless it was a dire emergency, and that Maggie should be able to reach him at his home. But he wasn't at the condo. Or else he wasn't answering the phone when Maggie was the caller.

And this after two weeks of silence.

She'd heard nothing directly from him. She'd returned, not knowing his decision regarding their marriage. And, of course, *he* had no idea at all that she and the children were back. Which left Maggie alone with three children to face the house and its memories. She had no idea how they'd react.

"There's the river down there," Daniel shouted. "Does that mean we're on the Sure-kill?"

"Yes, this is the *Sckuykill* Expressway."

"Uncle Trent calls it the Sure-kill Distressway," Rachel added, "but I don't think it's so funny anymore."

"I'm sure he doesn't, either," Maggie said, then gritted her teeth. Uncle Trent again. Children were so easy to read. Rachel and Daniel and even Grace in her limited capacity had talked incessantly about their uncle in the last several days. His absence was clearly noted, and it just as clearly caused worry. He'd checked in on Mickey, calling to talk to the boy's doctors and Mickey himself every other day, but there'd been not a word for Maggie.

He didn't return her calls, either. When the offers of help had come from the Shriners organization for Mickey to enter their new facility in North Philadelphia, and from Angel Flight East for their transportation, she'd called Trent all weepy and grateful. It had been such a weight off her shoulders and such a tremendous answer to desperate prayer that she hadn't been able to help the frequent breaks in her voice. All he had done in response was to say a few stiff words, and to contact the Florida doctors to help coordinate Mickey's eventual move.

Didn't he realize the strain all this had been? *Maybe not,* a quiet voice argued. She certainly hadn't understood what it would take to just start her day at seven making breakfast. After feeding and dressing three children, it was off to the hospital. And even that was complicated. She had to shepherd all the children to the car, get two buckled in their seats and Grace in her safety seat, then drive to the hospital. In the parking lot, it started all over again. The walk into and through the hospital, keeping track of them, was complicated as well. And now after two weeks alone, she was tired and scared that it might continue that way for the foreseeable future.

And what would she face when she reached the house? When she'd been there last month, the kitchen had looked like a war zone, but Michael had done wonders by her last visit, a week before they left on vacation. It was just that the house needed so much more. Maggie had never understood how Sarah had kept her sanity while dealing with a house that looked for all the world as if it were in the middle of being torn down.

"Aunt Maggie, do you know about the water?" Daniel asked.

Maggie started at the sound of his voice. "The water in the river?" she asked.

"No, silly, the water at our house. You said we were still going to live there, right?"

"We're almost there. What about the water?"

Rachel sighed. "It was just that Daddy didn't know. But Mommy wasn't mad," she was quick to reassure Maggie.

Maggie didn't feel reassured. Instead she had a sinking feeling in the pit of her stomach. "Daddy didn't know what?"

"About the old heater. We just camped. You know."

Maggie didn't camp. Had never ever wanted to camp. Couldn't imagine anything worse than camping with little children all under the age of nine. "Camped?"

Was that a squeak in her voice?

"Yeah, like when we go camping and Mommy and

Daddy cook the water for dishes. We have to cook it at home, too. Just like camping! But just 'til the new heater is hooked up, Daddy said.''

"Sarah, you were amazing," Maggie whispered, and prayed for strength.

The house came into sight just then. It sat high on a rise at the end of a drive that was several hundred yards long; it seemed to peer imperiously down the hill at them through two eyebrow windows cut into the roof. Michael had called the house a "grand old lady." To Maggie, the peeling paint and half-finished porches made it look more like a derelict. But although the house looked less than inviting to her, it was home to these children, and Maggie would do nothing to change their perceptions of it.

She stopped the van in front and started to set the brake.

"Um, Aunt Maggie," Rachel said, her voice hesitant, "I think maybe we should go in the back door."

Maggie hated to ask the obvious question, but it just seemed to pop out anyway. "Why?"

"'Cause Daddy finished undoing the front of the house."

Maggie gulped. "Undoing?"

"The old walls and the floors," Rachel answered.

"And the steps," Daniel chirped. "Don't forget he pulled down the old rickety steps."

Don't jump to conclusions, Mag old girl. They're only little. They probably don't mean it the way it sounds. Besides, you were here a week before they left. And anyway, he couldn't have taken out the heater, taken down the walls and stairs and torn out

*the floors. There'd be nothing left! He couldn't!
Could he?*

Maggie forced herself to put the car in park and to
stomp down on the parking brake. "I only have a
front door key, kids. It's this way or the highway."

"We were just on a bunch of highways," Daniel
complained. "I want to get out and ride my Big
Wheel."

Maggie chuckled as she turned off the car. "That's
sort of an old expression my grandfather used. 'It's
my way or the highway,' he always said."

"What's it mean?" Daniel demanded.

Maggie shrugged. "This way or forget it, I guess,"
she said, a little distracted as she unbuckled Grace
from her car seat.

"That doesn't make sense," he grumbled. "Why
are big people always using old sayings that don't
mean what they say they do? I think it's a 'spiracy
to keep kids from being too smart."

"Oh, no. Here we go again," Rachel groaned and
rolled her eyes.

Too late Maggie remembered Daniel's penchant for
needing to know the literal meaning in everything he
heard. "We'll sort it out later, Daniel. Right now
Grace needs a nap, and I think you could use a little
lie-down, too."

Grace perked up, and her eyes opened from their
half-mast position. "Not tired," she chirped, then ru-
ined her lively pretense with a wide yawn.

Maggie tapped Grace's little nose. "Careful before
you catch a fly in that mouth."

"Where's a fly?" Daniel asked.

Maggie laughed and changed the subject. "Let's get a move on, everybody. Into the house. We'll worry about the luggage later."

They proceeded as always with the routine Sarah had used, and which Maggie had adopted. She took Grace's hand, Rachel took Daniel's and they walked across the yard, up the steps and up to the front door. Maggie unlocked the door, opened it and peeked in. She stifled a gasp.

Rachel and Daniel had been alarmingly close in their description of Michael's latest demolition. The only thing left of the interior front of the house were studs, subflooring and the central staircase horses. Wires hung everywhere. There were holes here and there in the subflooring. She couldn't take the children in there! It was a minefield.

Maggie felt Rachel tug on her sleeve. "You want me to go and open the door? Mickey did it for Mommy. I'll be careful and not touch a thing, and I'll watch out for the holes."

Just then, however, the door from the kitchen pushed open and a man in jeans and a dark T-shirt came toward them. Dust motes floated in the sunlight between them. "Maggie? What are you guys doing here?"

Maggie squinted. The voice was Trent's, but it couldn't be him. He walked closer, and she backed up onto the porch. It was, of course, Trent, but his black hair was dusty and mussed. There were streaks of dirt on his shirt and jeans and on his forehead behind an errant lock. Maggie had never seen him so disheveled. Or so masculine. If this was indeed Trent, he should have gotten into jeans and T-shirts years ago.

"Trent?" she said foolishly, forgetting that she was supposed to be angry at him.

He followed her gaze to his clothes and shrugged. "They're Mike's. I didn't have anything to do this sort of work in."

"'This sort of work'?"

"I was putting in a new hot-water heater. It's all set."

His smile was boyish as if he were showing off a school project. Trent had put in a water heater? Maggie should have been relieved. There'd be hot water after all. But she knew Trent. *Lord,* she prayed, *tell me what to say.*

"By yourself?" she asked, trying to keep a neutral tone, still not sure whether to be proud or horrified. This was Trent. The same Trent who had tried to fix a leaking pipe in their first apartment with a wad of chewing gum.

"Yeah. And it wasn't too bad. Mike has the most incredible set of how-to books. I wanted to get more done before you got back. Why are you here? Why didn't you warn me? I could have met you at the airport. Is Mickey at Shriners already?"

If you'd called me even once in the last two weeks, you might know. She glanced at the children taking in their whole conversation and guarded her tongue. "He's all settled in. He still isn't bouncing back emotionally but he was ready to travel, so I decided it was time to come home. I left messages with our flight number on your answering machine and your voice mail. I even called Ellen. She said you were at home, but I didn't think of calling here." *I didn't know to call here,* she added silently.

Trent glanced at the children. Did he seem nervous? "Well, this is my home now too, right? I guess I should have had the phone company forward my calls here. You should do the same with your house."

"Uncle Trent, why did you have a different house from Aunt Maggie?"

"'Cause they're getting a divorce," Rachel informed Daniel. "Mommy explained all about it to me. But if Uncle Trent's moving here with us, how will you get divorced, Aunt Maggie?"

Maggie's gaze flew to Trent's. "We're not," Maggie said with false cheer. "Uncle Trent and I have been talking about getting back together. We sort of canceled the divorce. We're going to be your guardians together. Remember? We talked about this."

"But Uncle Trent never called us. He called Mickey. We thought he didn't care about us. I'm just a girl and so is Grace."

"And I'm just a little kid," Daniel added.

Now she knew she wasn't imagining Trent's fear of these children; there was such stark terror in the depths of his gaze that her heart shuddered. Then Trent dropped to one knee. Guilt had replaced the terror. "I love you all very much. I'm sorry you misunderstood. I didn't think how you'd feel not hearing from me. I'm so sorry. I was very upset by what happened to your daddy and mommy, and when I'm upset I work to help me forget. Unfortunately, that means I also forget things I shouldn't."

Rachel nodded sagely. "I heard Daddy say that to Mommy. He said you were sad about losing Aunt Maggie so you were working too much. It sounded very silly to me. You should have just asked us. Aunt Maggie wasn't really lost at all, cause we knew where she was all the time."

Trent looked up at Maggie. Two bright flags of red had appeared on his cheekbones. Rachel with her out-of-the-mouths-of-babes wisdom had clearly exposed a truth he'd rather have kept to himself.

Maggie tried. She tried *very hard* not to show any amusement, but her lips twitched. Trent glared. His obvious annoyance was a spark igniting the laughter that erupted from her chest.

Chapter Five

Trent stared up at Maggie, wishing a hole would open up in the earth and swallow him. Then her lips twitched, and his embarrassment turned into annoyance. He glared at her. Rather than take the hint that he didn't like her reaction, she started to laugh.

At him!

Her laughter sent his blood pressure soaring. How could she be so insensitive? How could she laugh at him in front of his nieces and nephew? Hadn't he suffered enough humiliation at her hands?

He shot to his feet and scowled down at her. It was easy for her to see only the humor in Rachel's innocent remark—after all, he'd been the one hurt. She'd left *him!*

He longed to shout, *You didn't have friends and co-workers treat you like you were made of spun glass the way they did me. I doubt your secretary brought you casseroles because she pitied you your lonely life.*

Maggie's voice penetrated the angry fog of his thoughts as she sent Rachel and Daniel back to the car for something. "No," she said, all laughter gone, her deep brown eyes as grave and sad as her tone. "I didn't have any friends left. They all reached out to you and turned their backs on me. Every one of them but Sarah and Michael."

It was only hearing her reply that made Trent realize he'd spoken his last thoughts aloud. Feeling his cheeks heat, and not wanting to think another second about how much more he'd exposed his inner feelings, he muttered, "I'll get washed up and bring in the luggage."

Ten minutes later Trent hoisted the last suitcase out of the back of the van. He turned toward a roaring sound coming down the drive and sidestepped just in time as Daniel careened around the back bumper on his Big Wheel, sliding into the spot Trent had occupied until a split second before. "Whoa, there, partner. Where's the fire?" Trent asked with a chuckle.

Daniel's eyes widened like saucers, and he did a comical double take. "How'd you know?"

"Know what?"

"Uncle Trent!" Rachel shouted from the front porch. "Help! Aunt Maggie started a fire!"

Trent didn't know he had the energy left to move as fast as he did. He dropped the suitcases, vaulting the porch railing a couple of seconds later. He followed Rachel and the trail of smoke to find Maggie in the kitchen ineffectively beating at flames with a towel. They surrounded and shot from a pot on the stove, leaping dangerously. Luckily he knew exactly where to find the fire extinguisher, and he had the flames out in a heartbeat.

Trent turned to Maggie to ask what had happened, but she was so pale and shaken that the question died on his lips. "Here. Sit down before you fall down," he said, taking her arm and helping her settle in a chair.

"I'm so sorry," she gasped. "I don't know what happened. All I did was put the potatoes into the hot oil. It took on a life of its own! I've never seen anything like it."

"They were frozen, Mag. You always make fresh. You have to sort of ease the frozen ones into the oil."

"How do you know that? Sometimes lately I feel so incompetent." She put her hand flat on her chest over her heart. "Goodness, my heart's still pounding."

Trent grinned. "I know because I did the same thing after I started cooking for myself. It didn't take long after you moved out for me to get sick of waiting for the delivery kid to bring my dinner. I've gotten pretty good at cheese steaks and frozen pizza."

"Well, I've lived my entire life not buying frozen potatoes and I think I'll go right back to old habits. I make fresh from here on," she said, sounding just a touch mutinous.

"Why'd you try frozen now? Like you said, you never did before, and your fries are great."

Maggie shrugged, looked guilty and checked the room—for little ears, he guessed. "Daniel doesn't like my cooking. He's always comparing the way Sarah did things to the way I do them. Then today he said that she always made them fries with their lunches. I thought it would take too long my way, and these were in the freezer.'' She shrugged. ''As I said, sometimes I feel so inadequate.''

For Trent, who was still trying to decide how close a relationship he wanted with Maggie, especially considering his earlier pique with her, it was a difficult moment. Part of him, the part still angry and hurt over her desertion, wanted to tell her that from now on she'd better be careful what she wished for because she just might get it—four times over. The other part wanted to reassure her, maybe give her a hug. He longed to feel her in his arms even if it was only to seek or give comfort, but he refused to think about why.

''Sarah's a hard act for anyone to follow,'' he said instead, hoping for middle ground. ''Don't stress over things like cooking as long as the kids get fed.''

''But I want to be a good mother for them. I want them to be happy again.''

''I know you do, and having a whole different set of adults taking care of them is not only new to them but may even be a little scary. But some new food isn't going to hurt them.''

Maggie sighed. ''But they don't laugh, Trent. Even Grace. I only get little smiles. Sometimes I'm tempted to just tickle the lot of them 'til they start laughing or crying. Just so they show some genuine emotion. Right now, I think all of them are just existing. Especially Mickey.''

"Daniel looked to be having a great time on his Big Wheel."

"Did he laugh?"

"Well, no. But he was coming to tell me you were burning the house down. It was exciting, but not a very funny situation."

Maggie frowned. "Now there's an idea. Why'd you put the fire out at all? Our troubles would be over. Paradise Found? They should have called it Stuck in Purgatory! Can't you see this refuge from the turn of the century reduced to smoldering rubble? I—'' Maggie gasped, shock and dismay reflected on her finely drawn features as tears flooded her eyes. "Oh, I can't believe I said that!"

It was those tears that had Trent reaching out to comfort her. He put his hand on her shoulder, determined to do no more than give her a reassuring pat. "It's okay. The condition of the house was a shock to me, too. But you'll see. It won't take all that long to put it all to rights. I'll probably have most of it done by Christmas."

She sniffled. "You?"

"I'm going to do it myself. Just the way Mike planned to. He did the work by himself. This place was his grand old lady. And he really did see this as paradise. Everywhere I look I see his hand, his plans. I have to finish it for him."

"But you don't do this sort of thing. Trent, you don't know the first thing about renovating a house. Last I heard you didn't even know how to fix a leaking faucet."

Trent bristled. "I'm learning. Mike didn't know any of this, either, when he started."

Maggie nodded and smiled. He wished it didn't look as if it took her so much effort. "You're right, of course. And you did get the hot-water tank in."

"Right." *And it only took three times as long to do it as the book said. At this rate this house will take me years.*

"Could we at least have some peanut butter and jelly sandwiches," Daniel said. His voice was the wrong side of a whine for Trent's liking. "I'm starved. Mom always made lunch on time."

Maggie jumped up. "Oh, of course. I'm so sorry, Daniel. It'll only take me a minute."

Trent leaned back against a counter and watched Maggie bustle around making lunch. Something about Daniel's attitude just didn't sit right, but he couldn't put his finger on why. "Hey, I'll have one of those while you're spreading," he told Maggie. "Let me give you a hand. Juice all around?"

Maggie shot him a grateful smile. "It's never that easy. No one ever wants the same thing to drink. You'd better ask them. Would you mind getting them to the table? It would be a big help."

Trent stared across the fields, watching the sunset. He leaned back in the porch swing and closed his eyes. Setting the swing in motion, he tried to drift without thinking. He was tired but it was a good kind of tired—the kind that settled on you after a hard day's work that was full of accomplishments. He knew Maggie was tired, too, but *her* tired came from stress and worry—and, he was afraid, near exhaustion. He wished he could feel triumphant over her apparent inability to completely cope with her new role, but watching her struggle and refuse to admit defeat tugged at his heartstrings.

He knew his decision regarding the path their marriage would take from here wouldn't ease her mind. But he had to protect himself from further heartache while still protecting the children from his parents. And moving into the apartment over the carriage house was the best solution he could come up with.

As if conjured by his thoughts, Maggie pushed open the kitchen door and came out onto the porch carrying a tray. She inhaled deeply. "Um. Smell that honeysuckle."

"Mike transplanted a bunch of it from the woods to climb along the rear border fence."

"I've always thought this was a wonderful place for children to grow up. Think of the adventures Mickey and Rachel have already had in those woods and in that tree house Michael built for them. They have so much more fun ahead, and so do the other two. I want that so badly for them."

Trent remembered how discouraged she'd been about the kids earlier, and knew that any minute now he was going to make her feel just as discouraged about their marriage. He wanted to soften the blow, so he put off the inevitable a little longer. "Speaking of Mickey," he said as she bent and offered him a glass of lemonade. "He missed you when I went to see him this afternoon. You've become very important to him."

Maggie sank into the wicker rocker and set her glass on the matching table next to it. "Your calls while he was in the hospital in Florida meant a lot. He was always a little brighter after them. I confess, I coveted some of that attention for myself as much as the other children did."

He sighed. *Some things just won't wait.* "I couldn't talk to you then, Maggie. I wasn't trying to hurt you. I just needed time to think about everything. About us. About where we're headed from here. I don't want to hurt you now."

She stiffened, obviously braced for bad news. "Then you decided against Ed's advice? Your parents meant what they said," she warned.

Maybe his compromise wouldn't be too disappointing to her after all, considering what she obviously thought he was about to say. "I know they meant it, Mag. That's why I came up with a compromise. I moved into the carriage house apartment. Sarah's mother and yours came over. They took care of Sarah's things in the studio and in the master bedroom, and I went through Mike's. The bedroom is cleared out, but it'll only be me in there. If there's a problem when I'm not over here, just call my cell phone and I'll be right over to help."

Trent was surprised to see anger blaze in her eyes. "So you aren't even going to let me have a chance to make things right between us. We're supposed to live separate lives except when the children are awake? Are you planning to come home for dinner, do whatever around here in the evenings, then vanish as soon as they're asleep? What about me, Trent? Am

I supposed to do your laundry, too, besides cooking your meals?''

Trent frowned. Was he treating Maggie like a live-in maid and nanny? "I hadn't thought of it that way," he admitted. "I thought that this way we could see where we go from here without either of us having too high an expectation. I'm just not ready to be that close to you yet—sharing a room, a bed. I need the space, Mag.''

A look of deep sadness suddenly drowned the anger in Maggie's big brown eyes, and nearly buckled Trent's resolve. She looked down at her lap, then back up—sadness replaced by a resolve of her own. "How much space? I hurt you badly, Trent, and I want to make amends. But that doesn't mean I'll be your doormat.''

"That isn't what this is all about. Look, I'll cook once in a while. And I'll do my own wash.''

"I'm not talking about housework! I'm talking about Nadine Morresey. I want some assurance that you're trying to resolve our problems. As long as you're still dating another woman, I can't see much hope for us.''

"I've already told her that you and I have decided to try making our marriage work. I haven't seen her since the memorial service.''

Maggie sighed and looked off at the sunset. "Then I don't see how I can deny you the space you say you need.'' She turned to look at him, her eyes sadder still, her brow furrowed with concern. "But I worry that your living in the carriage house will affect the children badly.''

He'd worried about the same thing. "If it does, we'll go with some other plan. This isn't necessarily permanent. It's just to give us a chance to move a little more slowly than we've been allowed to do so far. Every decision we've made has needed to be split second, including getting back together. Yes, we have to protect the children, but I think we have to be happy together for them to be happy. Don't you? And right now I'm barely comfortable sharing a dinner table with you, let alone a bedroom. If you're honest with yourself, I don't think you are, either."

Maggie stood and walked toward the back door, but she stopped on the threshold. When she looked back, her expression was incredibly soft and even a little sensual. "I'm entirely comfortable with you anywhere, Trent. But I can wait." Her chin went up a notch. "And I *will* wait as long as I have to, because we belong together. I believe it's the Lord's plan for us to be together, but I didn't listen to Him. I tore us apart. I'll find some way to show you how right our marriage is, how much you still need me. That's important to me. *You're* important to me."

She was gone before he could even think of a response. In fact, even when he thought of a reply, it was a childish lie. He wanted to shout that he didn't need her—didn't love her. But he knew he couldn't resist or deny the love for her that he'd buried deep in his heart—the love that just wouldn't die. The love that sooner or later he'd have to admit to them both.

Getting to his feet, Trent realized that the tiredness that had felt so good before he'd told Maggie of his decision no longer felt quite so satisfying. Now he just felt battered by life.

He headed toward the workshop and put the tools he'd used during the day back where they belonged. It was a ritual he'd begun a week earlier on the day he'd decided to finish Mike's work. His brother had been nearly fanatical about keeping his workshop in order, and to leave it a mess felt like a crime.

There was a strange side effect to all the manual labor he was doing. It was one thing he'd learned quickly. When you worked with your hands, your mind had time to think. And thinking too deeply was something he'd avoided his entire life.

In boarding school he'd signed up for every sport, club and committee he could fit into his schedule. He'd done the same thing in college and again in graduate school. With his busy life he'd avoided a lot of painful hours of thinking. He hadn't had time to be lonely for his family. He hadn't had time to re- member all he was missing by being so far away from home. It quickly became a habit that extended to avoiding self-examination, as well.

After college he'd bulldozed through life putting one foot in front of the other, never looking back but never looking toward the future, either. He'd made business plans but never personal ones. He'd met and married Maggie because he loved her to distraction— but he'd never really thought it out.

Then had come the moment when a discouraged, heartbroken Maggie had brought up the idea of adop- tion. Again, he hadn't thought. The niggling fear that he wouldn't make a good father had grown in him quietly, insidiously. And he'd realized it in that blinding moment of clarity. Grasping on to the only excuse open to him, he'd declared that he didn't believe in adoption. That he'd never raise another man's child.

And he'd stuck with his story for years while he pushed forward on a treadmill of his own making. He'd ignored Maggie's unhappiness, until seemingly without warning—though now he knew there had been plenty—she'd left.

And he'd seen what his stand had done to both of them.

But did he stop, take stock, think about his future or the mistakes of the past? No!

Again, he'd pushed on. He'd been lonely, so he'd started dating, never giving a thought to the fact that his divorce wasn't final. He'd filled every hour with work, concerts, plays, cocktail parties and fund-raising dinners. But he never, ever let himself think about his life—where it was going or where it had been.

When Maggie had begged for reconciliation, he hadn't considered her request for even a second. He'd told her they were better off apart and had dismissed her time and again. He'd thought he was trying to protect her, but seeing her tonight, her pain, the way she pointed the finger of blame at herself alone, he knew he'd been lying to himself. It was easy to do if you never stopped to contemplate your actions.

The truth was that it had been himself he was trying to protect, and it still was. But now he wasn't sure it was worth the price. He was here in the carriage house facing another lonely night. Another lonely night in a lonely bed with Maggie just across the yard in hers. And the worst part was that he knew he was welcome anytime he decided to take a chance on resuming their marriage.

But as much as he wanted Maggie in his arms and in his bed, he wasn't ready to forgive her for leaving, or to take a chance on being hurt again.

Chapter Six

Maggie walked into what was to be her new room. The beautiful mahogany Victorian bedroom suite had a Caribbean influence. She and Sarah had enhanced that feeling with yards of soft netting draped as curtains, swags and a loose flowing canopy. The walls were covered in a creamy beige, woven-grass wallpaper, adding to the Caribbean theme.

She loved this room, and it didn't bother her at all that it had been Sarah and Michael's room. In fact, it was a comfort to be here. She felt closer to them here where they had shared so much love and happiness. Knowing they were happy with the Lord now had already helped dull her grief a little, and she knew that they would want those they'd left behind to celebrate their lives rather than dwell on their untimely deaths.

But the room didn't feel quite right she thought. And as she sank down onto the high four-poster bed, she knew why that was. The room had been designed for two. For love. For romance. It wasn't a room to be alone in, and the very atmosphere reminded her that she was alone. And lonely. But that was what her life was right now. Lonely.

Oh, she had the children to fill her days, and she knew that taking care of them would keep her busy until well into each evening. But there was always this solitary time at the end of each day. It was a time during their marriage when she and Trent had always discussed their respective days. When she'd pictured them as parents, she'd seen this as the time when she would share the funny things, the heart-tugging things, even the maddening things their children had done during the day. Since leaving Trent, it was the time of the day when she'd missed him the most, and that had never been more true than since the children had come into her life. And now he was back, but not in the way she needed.

Maggie stood and went to the window facing the carriage house as a damp, late-summer breeze wafted into the room, stirring the gauzy curtains. As she looked into the open window of the carriage house, Maggie saw Trent pace a few times before he threw himself into a chair. Even from across the yard she could see the pent-up tension in his quick jerky movements, but she knew he didn't want her comfort. She was more than likely the cause of his stress.

Wrapping her arms about her waist, Maggie leaned her shoulder and head against the window frame. She desperately needed to feel Trent's arms around her right now to reassure her.

After several long minutes of deep thought as she stared across the yard and drive, Maggie unconsciously reached out to trace his beloved face, only to encounter the screen beneath her fingertips. She snapped back to reality.

He's so close, yet so far away. Lord, I know You have more for us than this. I know I have to wait, but I don't know how much longer I can do this alone. I need him. Please bring him back to me.

"You can endure all things through Christ who strengthens you," a quiet voice called from somewhere inside her. It was the verse that her pastor had given her when he'd called Florida to console her.

Maggie pursed her lips, and with one more glance at Trent, turned away to face the inevitable. She reluctantly moved toward the bed and climbed in. She had a long day ahead of her tomorrow. She needed her sleep.

But sleep was a long time in coming. Even when it did, she woke in tears several times during the night tortured by dreams of lost love and the hopeless feeling that she knew came because the pain she must endure was of her own making.

"I want waffles," Daniel whined. "I don't like pancakes."

"You do, too," Rachel shouted. "He does, too, Aunt Maggie."

"Do not!"

"Do, too!" Grace added.

A high-pitched whistle put an end to the cacophony. Maggie turned toward the noise to find Trent standing just inside the back door. Seeing him once again clad in rugged attire, formfitting blue jeans and a white T-shirt, her heart raced.

''Who likes pancakes?'' he asked, and Rachel and Grace shouted their support.

Daniel crossed his arms and scowled as an answer. ''The mes have it, Aunt Maggie. Today it's pancakes, one of my personal favorites,'' Trent confided to Daniel as he sat down next to him and ruffled his auburn hair. ''Maybe the next time she has the time to make a special breakfast like this one, she'll make waffles. Another of my personal favorites,'' Trent added with a grin and a wink to Maggie.

Maggie's stomach did a somersault. She turned away, flustered, telling herself it meant nothing that their first meeting had begun with just such a teasing gesture. Because unless something had changed since last night, this day wouldn't end with dinner, dancing and a good-night kiss on the cheek.

''So what are your plans for today?'' she asked him.

''The guy who promised to give Mike a hand with the heater called. He's coming by.''

''The heater? We don't need heat. Why don't you concentrate on putting the front rooms back together? There's no room to even walk in the family room, and I live in fear that Grace will get past me and into that area.''

''Can't,'' he said around a piece of pancake.

Rachel's brown eyes widened. ''Uncle Trent. You aren't supposed to talk with anything in your mouth.''

"Girls are so dumb!" Daniel pronounced. "He has to talk with his teeth and tongue in there, you know."

"You know I meant food, dummy!" Rachel yelled.

"Aunt Maggie asked him a question. How was he 'sposed to answer?"

"He could have waited to answer," Rachel retorted.

Trent swung his head back and forth from one child to the other, looking like a spectator at Wimbledon. "Time!" he said at last, his mouth empty but for his teeth and tongue. "I really think we need some rules here. First one. No arguing at the table. Everybody agree?"

Daniel and Rachel were clearly shocked at the idea of rules or agreeing to abide by them. Maggie knew it was a new idea, because though Sarah and Michael had been wonderful parents, they were lenient at times.

"What's a rule?" Daniel asked.

"Something you either always have to do or it's something you must never do," Maggie explained.

Daniel and Rachel looked blankly at the adults who had taken over their world. "Like..." Trent hesitated, thinking, "you have to brush your teeth before bed and in the morning. And you shouldn't fight with your sisters, especially at the table where you'll ruin everyone's meal. Aunt Maggie works hard to cook for us. We shouldn't ruin her meal with bickering. That sounds fair, doesn't it?"

Maggie watched the byplay and wondered, not for the first or even the hundredth time, why Trent was so convinced he didn't want to be a father. He was so good at it!

It was several hours later that Maggie pulled up her mother's long drive. Maggie's mother, Ester, and Sarah's mother, Nancy Merritt, were out on the front lawn waiting for the children. Nancy was no longer a maid, but her mother's friend and companion. Their relationship had changed over the years from employer and employee to friends. Her mother had taken on a caregiver's role for her former maid after Nancy collapsed and was diagnosed with a serious heart condition.

It was because her condition had been aggravated by the news of the accident that Nancy hadn't been able to travel to Florida to be with the children. This was the first time she'd see them since losing Sarah.

The two older women were sitting in the shade of the towering old elm tree, one of a few still alive in the Philadelphia area. Hanging from one of its tall limbs was a tire swing just waiting for the children. Under the same tree, on a similar swing, Maggie's lifelong friendship with Sarah had begun nearly thirty years earlier.

It was clear by the way the older women stood and waved that they were both waiting anxiously for the same thing: their grandchildren.

"Mom-mom! Grandmom!" the children shrieked as they spilled out of the van. Maggie unbuckled Grace from her car seat and put her on the ground, then grabbed the bag that held emergency clothing changes for all three before heading across the lawn.

Even from a distance Maggie could see that as Rachel and Daniel went into their grandmother's embrace, it was a tearful reunion. Ester soon had Grace in her lap, and it seemed that to the little girl this was just another visit. Maggie didn't know whether to be relieved or concerned that Grace had already begun to forget her parents and the tragedy of their passing.

By the time she reached the two older women under the tree, it was Maggie's turn for a hug. To her everlasting chagrin, her eyes filled with tears. She blinked furiously, trying to stem their flow, but Grace, who was talking more every day, blew the whistle, so to speak. "Why Aunt Maggie crywin'?" she asked.

Both Nancy and her mother pulled back, and the looks of love and support on their beloved faces opened the floodgates that Maggie had kept tightly locked for weeks. She felt her face crumple along with her control.

"Oh, dear," Nancy whispered, then gathered the children around her. "Suppose we go in and see how the cookies we baked this morning taste along with a big cold glass of milk?"

The children followed Nancy toward the back of the house. Considering the older woman's great loss, her kindness and understanding only made Maggie grow more weepy. Her mother enfolded her in her embrace once again, and they sank together onto the bench under the tree. No force on earth, especially Maggie's crumbling reserve of strength, could have held back the force of her tears. In seconds she began to sob openly. Unfortunately, her tears weren't the healing kind, but the sign of a breaking heart.

When Maggie ran out of tears, Ester cupped her daughter's face in her aging hands. Maggie looked into her mother's round face. "I'm sorry."

"For what? Being human?"

"But I cried in front of the children."

Ester's brown eyes, so like Maggie's own, widened exaggeratedly. "Oh! Horrors. Now they know you're human."

Maggie felt a helpless grin curve her lips. "I don't know what happened. Being hugged just felt so good. And then everything I've been feeling these last weeks all bubbled to the surface."

Her mother eyed her with a penetrating look. "Why aren't you getting hugs from Trent?"

"Trent keeps his distance from me," Maggie answered with a shrug that failed to lend the casual air she'd hope it would to her admission.

Ester's gaze sharpened. "So he really moved into that carriage house apartment. Nancy thought he might. He's turned out to be a carbon copy of Royce Osborne, with a few of his mother's character flaws thrown in for bad measure."

"No, he isn't like either of them at all," Maggie protested. "Michael's death has been hard on him, and you keep forgetting that I hurt him."

"He hurt you, too. He denied you children for years. Is that what all this is about? He's still piqued that you left to give him a wake-up call!"

Maggie shook her head. "I didn't tell him that when I walked out. I didn't even consciously know it myself 'til later. How was *he* supposed to know what I didn't even see? He's hurt. I wouldn't call what he's exhibiting a fit of pique. I don't think this will blow over quite so easily. Especially since I also think he resents being pushed into a corner. A week before the accident he told me to leave him alone. Nothing angers him more than to be forced into a position, and he *was* forced.''

''So he had to take you back and had to compromise on raising someone else's children.'' Maggie nodded and watched her mother's eyes spark. ''I suppose Michael let that truck driver hit them just to inconvenience Trent Osborne!''

''Mom! That's a terrible thing to say. It isn't like that. *He* isn't like that. Michael's death devastated him. And he's been very gracious about all this, considering. He says he just needs time, and I'm trying to give it to him.'' Maggie frowned, wishing she could understand Trent's inner feelings. ''He's so good with the children. You should see them together. He loves them so much. You should have seen him when Albertine and Royce came to the hospital. He was like a mother bear defending her cubs when they said they wanted the children. It's weird, but I'd swear he's afraid of those kids sometimes. Then other times, he says or does just the right thing as naturally as if he were a born father.''

''But how is he with you?''

''Distant. Sometimes angry.'' Maggie narrowed her eyes, considering. ''Confused, too, I think.''

''And you still love him no matter what?'' her mother said.

Maggie nodded. "That won't ever change. All I have to do is look at Albertine and Royce and I understand every one of Trent's faults. Except his stand on adoption. That I've never understood, but Ed Hanson says a lot of men feel the same way. Of course, that doesn't really matter anymore, does it?"

"You aren't feeling guilty, are you?"

"Occasionally," Maggie said with a self-conscious shrug. "I'm alive and Sarah's not. I'm enjoying her children, Sarah's not. Oh, Mom." Maggie sniffled and reached for the tissue her mother held out. "I miss her so much!"

"Grief fades, darling. You still miss your father, don't you? But not every single minute anymore. Right? You just hang in there and come here if you need a hug. With you loving him, one day Trent's going to wake up and see what a gem he has in you."

Maggie gave her mother a watery smile. "Maybe you're just a mite prejudiced, Mom."

"Just exactly the way you've always been about those children. You're going to be a wonderful mother to them." Ester squeezed Maggie's hand. "Come on. Let's go see what Nancy's up to with those grandchildren of ours. By the way, how's the house coming along? Nancy and I were horrified when we saw it last week. Apparently Michael had been busy right before they left."

Maggie chuckled. "I imagine you two felt somewhat like I did when I walked in there yesterday." Maggie held the screen door into the kitchen area open for her mother, then finished her explanation. "It looks like a bomb went off. Trent says tearing it all out and putting it back right is probably the fastest way to go about it. Unfortunately, there are a bunch of children living in the midst of the chaos.''

''He mentioned his plan to Ester and me.'' Nancy bit her lip before going on. ''He could have done it,'' she said, sounding as proud of Michael as his own mother should have. ''But can Trent? I didn't know he was handy around the house. I always pictured him as the type to hire workmen.''

''He is.'' Maggie giggled, then tried to describe the look on the plumber's face when he saw the chewing gum wadded on the leaking pipe in their apartment.

''This could get interesting,'' Ester said with a dry chuckle. ''Remember you and the children can always come stay here if he blows the house up or floods you out.''

Maggie blushed. ''Actually, it was me who almost burned the house down.'' She went on to share the story of the French fry fire, as well as several other outrageously funny problems her inexperience with children had caused thus far.

By the time she was on her way to visit Mickey with Nancy, her mother had Grace down for a nap and had started doing crafts with Daniel and Rachel. Though her mother would never have grandchildren of her own, she had been a doting grandmother from the day Mickey was born.

Maggie and Nancy were both anxious to see how Mickey was responding to his new environment. They entered the room to find him staring out the window, ignoring the TV that was set to his favorite Saturday cartoon.

"Who could this handsome lad be?" Nancy asked. "Could this be my grandson? Goodness, it is!"

"Hi, Grandmom. You didn't have to come, you know."

"Michael Trenton Osborne! What a thing to say! As if I'd need duty to make me come see my own grandchild."

Mickey shrugged. "It's not like we can have fun or anything. All I can do now is lay here."

"Oh? And how would you know that? I hear that pretty soon you'll be good as new."

"Yeah. Sure. How are the other kids, Aunt Maggie? Rachel really misses Mom, I'll bet. You, too, I guess. Uncle Trent misses Daddy. He really loved him, you know."

Maggie nodded, wishing she could climb into Mickey's head and know what was going on in there. "How about you?" she asked, hoping to draw him out. "Do you miss them?"

A rebellious look came into Mickey's eyes. His chin firmed stubbornly. "I'm glad they aren't here because having me be crippled would have made them sad."

Shocked at first, Maggie quickly regrouped. "If they were here, they would tell you that you're not crippled. You were hurt and your body has to have time and help to repair itself. You *will* walk again. And they'd want you to believe that. *We* want you to believe that."

"I still miss them a whole lot," Mickey admitted.

"And I know that makes you sad, and that's okay. You realize that, don't you?" Nancy asked.

"Yeah. Uncle Trent told me it was okay to be sad. So did Aunt Maggie. That's what I decided to be today—sad."

Nancy smoothed a stray lock off Mickey's forehead. "Do you want to play a game? I'm sure there are some games in the playrooms. Suppose Aunt Maggie goes there and finds one?"

Mickey shook his head and handed his grandmother a book. "Could you just read to me? I'm sort of tired."

"Well, sure. We'll take turns."

Maggie stepped back to watch Mickey as Nancy read to him, but within a few minutes he was asleep. Or he appeared to be. After an hour they left, disappointed and worried about a child whose once-exuberant personality now seemed a distant memory.

Mickey opened his eyes and pursed his lips, fighting tears as he heard the door swish shut. He loved Aunt Maggie and Grandmom, but he wished they wouldn't keep lying to him. He knew he was broken and that nobody wanted a broken kid. He knew he wouldn't get better no matter how hard he tried. He knew he'd never get better because his grandparents had said so. He'd have to live in a place for crippled kids. They had the place all picked out where he'd have to go live. Because he'd be a burden unless he was in an institution.

Mickey hadn't been at all sure what *burden* or *institution* meant after he heard his daddy's parents talking outside his hospital room back in Florida. But he'd asked a volunteer there. And now he knew. He didn't like the sound of an institution, but he liked being a burden even less.

Chapter Seven

Trent turned off the table saw and cocked his head, listening. High-pitched squeals and raucous shouts reached his ears a few seconds later. Maggie was back from her mother's with the kids, he mused, and smiled as he heard her shout for order. She was apparently organizing a game of some sort. He chuckled. She hadn't yet figured out that order was the last thing you got when three children under nine played any game. A few minutes later, though, the shouting turned a little too frantic for his liking and he was off like a shot to investigate.

He blasted out of the shop door and came to a screeching halt. Grace stood in the middle of the lawn, facing him with a carefree grin on her face. Behind her, Maggie wore a worried frown. She looked like a statue, pale as marble and still as stone.

"Kitty," Grace shouted gleefully to Trent.

At that point, he looked more closely at the bundle

of black-and-white fur in her arms. Some days it just didn't pay to get out of bed. He put a hand up traffic-cop style to Maggie, never taking his eyes off Grace and her troublesome armful. "Stay there, Mag. I'll handle it from here. Grace, love, that isn't a kitty," he told the toddler.

Grace's grin turned into a frown. "Pretty kitty my *fwend!*"

"Honey, I'm sure he's very nice, but that isn't a kitty. He's a wild animal. A skunk." Trent knew that if the animal were any older, the toddler would already know how true that was. Luckily, the skunk looked content and might not scratch her—or worse, bite her. Any danger of it spraying was minimized by the way she held it with its tail tucked under its bottom. Unless she lost her grip. Then things would get interesting—fast.

"Want to pet my kitty, Uncle Twent?" she asked. "His name is Bobo."

Trent sighed. *In for a penny.* He had to get close sooner or later—he may as well do it by invitation. He inched closer, careful not to startle the little animal or Grace. *How early do they learn to spray?* he wondered as he reached out to stroke the soft fur stripe on its back.

"Sweetheart, this is a skunk."

"Not a kitty?"

"No, and cute as he is, we can't keep him. It would be bad for him. He'd...ah...get sick from living with us. He needs his mommy."

Grace's lower lip puckered. "He not have a mommy. Just like me."

Trent felt his heart lurch and heard Maggie's quick intake of breath. He looked away from Grace for a moment. "Mag, get the others and get inside before they spook it." He turned his attention back to baby girl and baby skunk, picking up the conversation where it had left off. "Oh, his mommy died too? That's sad. But I'll bet he has lots of aunts and uncles. Animals have big families, you know. Suppose you and I go over to the woods and send him back home. Okay?"

Grace's face started to crumple. "Come on, Gracie, don't cry. You'll scare your little friend. Remember, he's a wild animal. He has to live in the woods."

"I want my kitty," she said, tightening her hold. The skunk gave an annoyed little squeal.

Desperate to get her to loosen her hold at least a little, he said the only thing he could think of. "Maybe we can get you a real kitty soon, but we can't keep Booboo. It wouldn't be fair."

Her hold loosened perceptibly. "He's Bobo, not Booboo!"

Trent winced at her raised voice. "Sorry. Bobo. Bobo has to go home now, Gracie. Come on, we'll take him home to his family."

Bottom lip puckered and quivering, Grace nodded and turned to toddle off toward the woods. Trent stayed close at her side, his mind searching for a way to ensure a safe release of her captive. He finally settled on helping Grace set the skunk on the ground while making sure she kept the tail tucked under. Trent hooked his arm around her waist and sprinted off with her as soon as the skunk's feet touched the ground.

The bumpy ride he gave her cradled against his chest had Grace laughing uproariously by the time he collapsed onto his back on the rear porch. His heart pounding, Trent gasped for breath as Grace crawled off him.

"Is everything safe?" Maggie asked as she stuck her head out the back door and sniffed.

Trent looked up. His already pounding heart turned over at the sight of her, and he could have sworn he felt the porch floor tilt under his back. She wore shorts and a tank top in deference to the warm late September day. How had he forgotten those lush curves, or how smooth and shapely her legs were? He knew when Maggie noticed his interest because a blush stole up her neck and across her sweet face.

It was that innocence that had first drawn him to Maggie so many years before, when she'd been a senior design student at Drexel University and he'd been finishing his postgraduate work at Stanford. They'd met at Christmas and had married six months later, after a pen pal courtship that adhered to the most old-fashioned of courting standards. And even after their honeymoon, she'd still somehow retained the innocence she'd given him on their wedding night.

When he glimpsed it, that sweetness had never failed to kindle his need for her and it didn't fail this time. He sat up and looked away, not wanting her to realize how much she still affected him.

Trent was grateful to Grace, who'd promptly pounced onto his back demanding another ride. He pulled her over his shoulder and into his lap, his wits finally together enough to answer Maggie's question. "Everything's okay. Bobo's on his way back home to his aunts and uncles," he explained. "They take care of him just the way we take care of Gracie. Right, Gracie?"

Grace looked up at him with her big brown eyes. "And they love him, too! Right, Uncle Twent?"

His throat started to ache. He swallowed and nodded, answering with a hug. He was losing it. First, Maggie's return to his life had begun squeezing his heart mercilessly, then assaulting his senses. And now the kids started.

"Right. They love him, too," he answered, and nearly cringed at the rusty quality of his voice. He hoped Maggie would chalk it up to his sprint from the edge of the woods.

"Bobo wasn't a kitty," Grace told Maggie, her little face serious, her tone self-important with her new knowledge.

"No. He sure wasn't. It's a good thing he liked you. He was a skunk," Maggie said. Then she was telling Grace about the dangers and repercussions of approaching another such creature, and extracting a promise that she wouldn't approach any more wild animals.

"I pwomise," Grace said, then turned back to Trent. "Can we go get my kitty now?"

"Your kitty?" he asked, and for a few seconds was completely at sea. Then he realized she wasn't asking to go back to the woods to find good ol' Bobo. She was talking about his nebulous future promise of a kitten. "Oh! *That* kitty. I said maybe, Gracie. And I said soon. *Soon* doesn't mean right now. And *maybe* means...ah...means—"

"It means that Uncle Trent and I have to discuss it," Maggie said, coming to his rescue even though her expression promised later retribution. "And soon really has to mean later in this case. Like after the house is done. Remember all the holes in the floors and walls? Kittens are small and curious and would get into all those dangerous places. The house wouldn't be safe for a kitten right now. We wouldn't want it to get hurt—*if* we agree to get one at all. Okay? Why don't you run on in and watch the *Young Adventurers* video we got today with the other kids? Tell Rachel I said she should rewind it so you won't miss anything."

"You gonna talk about my kitty now?"

Maggie crossed her arms and leaned back against the house. "Oh, you can count on it," she promised Grace, who squealed with glee and ran into the house.

Trent winced as the screen door flapped shut in her wake, then got to his feet. At least he could face the music standing.

"How could you?" Maggie demanded.

"I only said *maybe*."

"*Maybe* from an adult means *yes* to a two-and-a-half-year-old. Trent, I have too much going on right now. I can't handle the addition of a kitten to the mix. And it wouldn't stop at that. Each of them would want a pet of their own. I shudder to think what Daniel would ask for."

"Well, I think we're safe from Tyrannosaurus

Rex,'' he teased, but didn't get a smile. He got a
glare. Trent was a little taken aback by the strength
of her anger. He'd been prepared for annoyed, but
this was more. ''I didn't know what else to do,'' he
defended himself. ''She was starting to hold on to the
thing for dear life. I was afraid if she squeezed any
harder the little guy might get scared and scratch her
or bite her. Then there was the charming possibility
that he'd wiggle his tail free and spray. I thought the
promise of a possible pet in the offing would be better
than rabies shots or tomato juice baths for both of
us.''

Maggie groaned and plunked down into one of the
wicker chairs. ''I'm sorry.'' She sighed and put her
head back with her eyes closed for a second or two,
her struggle to overcome her deep-seated tension evident. ''You're right,'' she said, looking over at him.
''We'll just put her off if she asks for a pet again.
Don't mind me.''

''What is it? Taking care of the kids getting to
you?''

She shook her head. ''I'm just so worried about
Mickey. What did you think of the way he acted when
you saw him yesterday?''

''He seemed tired. I imagine the trip was a lot for
him. He fell asleep right after I started reading to him.
I hung around for a few minutes, but he didn't wake
up. I thought I'd head in there again after dinner.''

''He was probably pretending to be asleep. I think
he did the same thing with Nancy and me this afternoon.''

''Why would he do that?''

Maggie shrugged. "I don't have a clue."

Now Trent was worried. "Maybe he doesn't believe he'll ever walk again. And he just lost his parents on top of that. It might be a good idea to have a psychologist talk to him."

"I don't know how he'd react to that. I know there's something that *we're* missing, but would a stranger see it if we can't? Do you think he'd even talk to a stranger if he won't talk to you or me or Nancy?"

"It's worth a try. When I'm in there tonight, I'll find out if there's someone on staff."

Maggie stood. "Okay. If you're comfortable with the idea. I guess it couldn't hurt. Are you eating here or are you going to grab something on your way to the hospital?"

Grace came barreling back out the door before he had a chance to answer. "Come kill de bug. You 'quash it dead! It's in our house."

Trent raised his eyebrows in a silent question.

"It's probably a mosquito or a fly," Maggie told Grace. "Or maybe a spider." Maggie chuckled at Grace's departure. "After the bugs in Florida, she's not exactly a fan of the insect kingdom. We had to make a rule that outside is the bug's house and that they're not fair game in their house. Inside, they are."

"I'll go. I know they aren't your favorite, either."

Maggie smiled. "After Florida, Pennsylvania's bugs are pretty tame, but thanks. So are you staying for dinner?"

Trent was surprised how much he wanted to say yes, but he still hesitated, thinking of his reaction to

Maggie. And then there was her accusation that he'd practically turned her into a maid and a nanny by staying in the carriage house. Since he wasn't ready to change things between them, he'd better back off a little, he decided. It was fast food for him again tonight.

"That's okay," he told her. "Mickey wasn't happy with his dinner last night. I thought I'd take him a kid's meal and eat with him. I'll be sure to mention a psychologist to the nurses. Right now, though, I have a search-and-destroy mission."

Trent watched Mickey pick at his favorite food after ignoring the toy inside the box. "Do you want me to put the toy together?" he asked the boy.

Mickey shrugged. "If you want," he said, his tone flat.

Trent frowned. Maggie was right. The kid wasn't acting at all like himself. "I hear you started therapy today," he mentioned, trying to sound nonchalant as he fitted slot *A* into slot *B* of the toy.

"Yeah. It was fine."

It didn't sound fine to Trent. "What did you do?"

"Nothin'. I just lay there, and they moved my legs. Kind of a waste if you ask me."

"You know you're going to get better, don't you?

Mickey shrugged. "Yeah. Sure."

He didn't sound sure to Trent. In fact, he sounded decidedly sarcastic. "Mickey, do you want to talk about what has you so down? I'd like to help. Really, I would. Is it your mom and dad? They wouldn't want you to stay unhappy. You know that, right?"

"Aunt Maggie read me all sorts of things about heaven one day in the hospital in Florida. It's okay that they left us to go there. I know they're happy."

"Do you miss being at home, then? You'll be home with us soon. All you have to do is get better enough to be released."

"Yeah. That's it," Mickey agreed, but to Trent it sounded as if the boy had just grabbed onto a lifeline. "And I'm tired," he added, and yawned expansively. "I think I'll go to sleep now. You can leave."

"I could read to you."

"Naw. That's okay. You can go help Aunt Maggie get the little kids to bed. I'm fine. It isn't too bad here. Really."

Trent felt once again a wrenching in his chest. It was clear the boy was troubled, and just as clear that Trent wasn't helping him. He knew it was ridiculous, but he felt rejected and inadequate—which was really nothing new at all.

Chapter Eight

Maggie put the last pot in the dish drainer and dried her hands on the kitchen towel. Arching her back to get the kinks out, she turned and surveyed the room. Everything was cleaned and spotless. She smiled when she looked at the clock. There were about ten or fifteen minutes left of the evening before she had to start the bedtime ritual of baths, pajamas and goodnight prayers. She was getting better at this!

"Hey, guys, how about a story?" Maggie asked as she walked around the half wall that separated the family room from the kitchen.

Daniel beamed a smile at Maggie as he ran to get the *Bible Storybook*. Rachel climbed up next to her as Grace came over to the sofa, a scowl on her little cherub face. "Lauk up dare," she said, and put her head back to stare up at the high ceiling.

Maggie looked, too. There was nothing up there.

''The spider's all gone. Uncle Trent killed it. Remember?''

''No! Lauk up dare!'' she demanded, temper showing in her now-red face. This time, Grace pointed to her nose as she tipped her head back.

''Are you saying *chalk? Chalk* up there?'' she asked.

Unfortunately Grace nodded vigorously, her bright curls bobbing. ''Waaay up dare.''

Maggie looked up Grace's tiny nose, and sure enough there was a white nub of chalk blocking her left nostril. ''Well, it certainly is chalk. I guess I'd better help you get it out of there.''

Grace nodded energetically again, and try Maggie did. She tried everything she could think of. And Grace was as cooperative as a squirmy two-year-old could be. But the chalk remained firmly lodged. Stymied, Maggie called the children's pediatrician, who suggested a quick, simple trip to the Emergency Room. Maggie sighed. She knew that a trip anywhere with three children was anything but quick or simple.

It took twenty minutes to pack up everything they'd need, scribble a note to Trent and get the three children into the van. Another fifteen went by before she reached her mother's, where she left Rachel and Daniel for the night in the care of Ester and Nancy. Then she had to backtrack to Paoli Memorial.

When Maggie pulled the van up to the ER entrance, Grace took one look at the big scary place and balked. But Maggie prevailed, and soon they were in a treatment room.

After a quick look, the doctor said that even though

it was no more than an inconvenience, the chalk had to come out. But Grace had exceeded her two-year-old's limit of patience with Maggie's probing back at the house. The staff was forced to strap her into a papoose board to immobilize her. That was when she proved the old adage about temper and red hair. It took two additional interns to hold her still enough for the doctor to work on the recalcitrant chalk.

"Mrs. Osborne, this just isn't working," Doctor Burns told Maggie as he wiped the sweat from his brow. "For right now, why don't we let her get quiet with you. Maybe you can help her relax."

Maggie turned toward the sound of hurried footsteps striding toward them. It was Trent, looking worried and fierce. "What's going on?" he demanded. "I could hear her screaming from the parking lot."

"Mr. Osborne, I'm Dr. Burns," the doctor said. The men shook hands, but Trent didn't lose the scowl. The doctor chuckled. "Calm down, Dad. We really aren't into torture here. Grace shoved chalk up her nose and we're having a rough time extracting it. Mostly because your daughter's stronger than she looks." He grinned. "The kid has a good set of lungs, too! My ears are ringing."

Maggie saw Trent take a mental step backward at the doctor's assumption that he was Grace's father. But then he blinked and looked over at Grace. "Uncle Twent," Grace sobbed. "Like my lauk. Take Gwace home now!"

Trent looked back to the doctor. "I'm guessing that's not an option."

The doctor shook his head. "I was just about to

tell Mom that it's got to come out of there. I've got
one more shot at it with a hooked forceps that I just
sent for. If that doesn't work, I'm going to have to
send her up to surgery. I don't think there's much of
a danger of her aspirating it, but it still has to come
out.''

Trent stepped next to the narrow bed. "I'm sorry,
sweetheart, the doctor has to get it out of there."

Just then, one of the interns came back with the
forceps he'd gone after. Grace took one look at him
and started screaming again. Trent jumped away from
the bed in shock. The intern fished a ball of sterile
cotton out of his pocket, and, with humor twinkling
in his eyes, handed it to Trent. "Here, try this. It
really helps. And while you're at it, would you help
hold her still?''

Trent looked from the cotton to Grace and back at
the intern. "I'll take the noisy end. It only seems
fair," he said, and grinned as he muffled her cater-
wauling with the cotton. "Geez, kid. You've got a
big mouth," he told Grace as he stepped to the head
of the gurney.

Grace miraculously stopped her screaming to stare
up at Trent. "Go home?"

"*After* the chalk is out. If you hold still, it won't
take long at all." He cradled her head in the palm of
one hand and cupped her forehead with the other.
"These guys are just trying to help you, sweetheart.
Let's see how still you can be."

Grace apparently took Trent at his word, because
even though she started shouting her indignation
again, she didn't move a muscle. And not a minute

later the chalk pulled free with the use of the new instrument.

Dr. Burns, whose son was born the same day as Grace, begged her not to be mad at him. Grace, with her newly found stubborn streak, folded her now-free, pudgy little arms and scowled. But then her sunny disposition shone through, and she gave wet baby kisses to all those she'd been terrorizing since her arrival. Trent scooped her up, and they followed Dr. Burns out of the examination room.

"You were great with her," Maggie ventured.

"He thought I was her father," Trent said, as Grace nestled her head against his throat. Maggie could see the confusion tinged with awe in his expression as he spoke of the doctor's misconception. Why couldn't Trent see what others did? That he loved Grace and the rest of the children as if they were his own. Again, Maggie wondered if fear, more than an abhorrence of adoption, had made him so stubborn on the subject.

She patted his shoulder. "You'll see, Trent. Pretty soon you'll find yourself believing it, too."

He sighed and dropped his cheek against Grace's silky curls. "I hope so, Mag. I sure hope so."

"Why do you doubt it?" she asked, as they stopped at the front desk and signed the release forms.

When they moved on, Trent picked up the conversation. "Maybe because I'm just not good with them. I didn't do very well with Mickey tonight. He pretended to be tired and asked me to leave."

Maggie narrowed her eyes and stared in disbelief at Trent as she held the outside door open for him. "I told you that Mickey did essentially the same thing to Nancy and me. It's no reflection on you. He's troubled right now. That's all there is to it.''

"After I left him, I talked to his doctor about a counselor. I hope Mickey'll talk to whomever it is. I'm afraid he won't get better with this miserable attitude of his. I tell you, Mag, I wish I could crawl inside that kid's head so I'd know what's going on in there.''

"I thought exactly the same thing," Maggie confided.

Trent ran his hand through his hair. She could almost see the wheels of his mind turning. "I'm sure he believed me when I first told him why he couldn't feel his legs. He understood that it would probably be a temporary problem. But now that he's starting to get feeling back, he's acting as if we're all lying to him.''

Maggie nodded, equally concerned. But she mentally put Mickey on another shelf in her mind. She'd ponder his attitude later. Right now she needed to deal with Trent and his. She could hear the frustrated love in his voice. She had to find a way to get him to not only accept his role in the lives of the children but to believe he could be what they needed.

Maggie unlocked the van, while Trent carefully placed Grace in her car seat. While he was occupied with buckles and snaps, Maggie cast her eyes heavenward. Her faith was new and she often forgot to pray, but whenever she remembered, life's problems miraculously became easier to handle.

Please, Lord, she prayed silently, *help me show him. Help me help him—help both of them.*

The answer came like a thunderbolt from above. She'd never been comfortable with Trent's idea of Mickey seeing a psychologist, and now she knew why! Mickey needed *their* help, not the help of a stranger. And Trent needed to be the one to help him. It was so clear that she felt foolish not to have thought of it sooner. Then she remembered her prayer and felt once again the utter peace her faith brought her. Her Lord really *was* in charge of everything.

"I'm still not sure Mickey needs a professional," Maggie told Trent, as she pulled on her sweater. "I think he needs you. Why not go see him tomorrow? Maybe the more time you spend with him, the better he'll get. Don't let him chase you away again. Tell him to take his nap and that you'll be there when he wakes up."

Trent stuffed his hands in his pockets. "I don't see why you think *I* can help."

Maggie shrugged and climbed into the van. "Because Mickey and your brother were very close, Trent, and I was there when you used to call him in Florida. I think you make him feel closer to Michael."

"Maggie, didn't you hear a word I said? I completely bombed with the kid. He sent me packing."

"Who's the adult here?" Maggie asked. "He can't really make you leave his room. You just stick to him like glue. Don't leave. Wear him down. Sooner or later, I bet he'll tell you what's eating at him. Then we'll ask someone who knows more than we do about kids how to handle whatever it is."

"Maybe you could do that. You're better with them than I am."

"Better?" Maggie shook her head. "How am I better? It seems to me that it was you who made order out of chaos at breakfast this morning. I was the one who let Grace get hold of that chalk. And let us not forget Bobo the skunk!"

"Kids get in all kinds of trouble. Do you have any idea how many hours Mike spent in that ER? I'm surprised they didn't know the Osborne name in there."

"Exactly my point," Maggie said, feeling and sounding just a touch triumphant. "You need to give yourself and these children a chance before you write off them or you. Go to see Mickey again tomorrow. Give it a chance."

Trent pursed his lips and stared at the ground for a long few seconds, then nodded. "Okay, I'll try. But don't be surprised if I make a mess of it."

Maggie smiled, relieved. "Just give it a shot. That's all any of us can do in life. Listen, why don't you leave your car here, and we'll pick it up on our way back from church tomorrow? Then you can go on to see Mickey from here."

"Church? Maggie, I don't think so. I'm trying as hard as I can to do what I'm supposed to do, but church just isn't for me. I know Mike was really into this religion stuff, but I don't need that sort of thing the way he did." Trent took a step backward and Maggie had to restrain herself from reaching out to him. Instead, she wrapped the fingers of one hand around the steering wheel and turned the key in the ignition with the other.

She was oh-so-tempted to tell him just how very much he did need it. He clearly didn't understand what she and Mike and Sarah had found at The Tabernacle—with their acceptance of Jesus Christ as their savior. *But he will,* she promised herself. She'd follow the advice Pastor Jim had given to the congregation when he talked about marriages where only one of the couple was a believer. She'd show Trent quietly by example what he could have if he just reached out for it. She wouldn't hound. She wouldn't lecture. She would just live her life and be the Lord's messenger with her witness.

"Okay. You don't want to go to church with us," she said, then realized that she wasn't ready to say good-night only to face the lonely ride home. "Suppose I drop you off here on our way to church in the morning? I'd appreciate the company on the ride home."

Maggie could see the wariness suddenly engulf Trent's eyes. It hurt, but she forced herself not to react.

"I don't think that's a good idea. It would probably wind up towed by morning. I'll follow you, and carry Grace inside for you," he promised.

Nodding, she bit back any further plea as he closed the door to the van. Finishing the race was all that mattered, she told herself as she watched him walk to his car. As long as Trent eventually came to trust her and want to be with her again, it didn't matter how long it took.

Even so, her heart was heavy some minutes later when Trent put Grace on her bed, then turned and left with only a good-night nod.

"Why didn't Uncle Trent come to church?" Rachel demanded as she climbed down out of the van into the church parking lot the next morning.

Maggie worded her answer carefully. She couldn't lie, nor could she tell Rachel that Trent didn't see the point in going to church. "He went to see Mickey this morning."

"Is Mickey coming home soon?" Daniel wanted to know.

"He'll be home as soon as he's strong enough," Maggie said.

"I'm going to pray that he'll be strong real soon, Aunt Maggie," Rachel said.

"Me, too!" Daniel echoed.

"Too!" Grace added, as they all approached the front door of the church.

"This is an enthusiastic group if I ever saw one," The Tabernacle's pastor exclaimed.

In his mid-thirties, Jim Dillon was tall, handsome and single. He was also the complete antithesis of what most people expected of the pastor of a large suburban church. Today, he wore a plaid dress shirt, black jeans and no tie—never a tie. He was a simple man with simple tastes. He still lived in a tiny apartment attached to the converted barn that made up the sanctuary and Sunday School rooms, and was thoroughly devoted to his parishioners. Many of the older women were forever trying to fix him up with their young relatives and acquaintances, but he always politely refused.

"We're going to pray for Mickey to come home soon," Rachel said as she broke ranks and ran forward to hug Pastor Jim, her hero.

"He's all settled at Shriners?" Jim Dillon asked Maggie.

"Uncle Trent's visiting him this morning," Daniel added.

"That's why Uncle Trent isn't here," Rachel went on. "You can meet him next week. He doesn't look like Daddy. He looks more like you."

"Is that so?" Pastor Jim asked, amusement making his green eyes sparkle.

Maggie grinned and teased. "You've met him. What do *you* think? Tall. Dark. Handsome."

"Maggie!" someone called from inside the church.

Turning toward the voice, Maggie waved. "Oh, there's Mrs. White," she told the children.

The older woman had a well-rounded figure, salt-and-pepper hair and the kindest smile this side of heaven. She was in charge of the two-year-old nursery room where her patience was much needed. Mrs. White rushed forward toward the children on surprisingly light feet. "How's my munchkin? Oh, I've missed you." She bent down and hugged Grace.

"I had lauk up dare," Grace proudly told her teacher.

"Chalk," Maggie clarified. She lifted Grace into her arms, needing once again to reassure herself that the toddler had suffered no ill effects from the har-

rowing night before. "I'll tell you later how she ter-
rorized the entire ER staff."

"Goodness, this must be such a difficult adjustment
for you, Maggie dear. Suppose I take the others to
their rooms for you so you can chat with Pastor Jim."
She clapped her hands then held them out to Grace.
The child giggled and dove from Maggie's arms to
Mrs. White's.

"So, what's the real reason Trent didn't come today?" Jim Dillon asked, as several other children fell
in behind Daniel and Rachel to follow Mrs. White as
if she were the Pied Piper.

Maggie felt a blush steal across her cheeks at his
question. "Trent doesn't think he needs 'religion,' so
he opted out."

Jim nodded. "I know how he perceives us. He said
much the same thing after the funeral, when I tried to
talk to him about Jesus. How are things between you
two?"

"Better than they were, but far from ideal," Maggie answered. She couldn't bring herself to explain
further, but she took comfort in Pastor Jim's promise
to pray for their marriage, and his offer of an ear if
she needed one.

Chapter Nine

Trent stopped at the entrance to the hospital the next morning and took a few calming breaths. He hadn't even been this nervous on his wedding day. What if he only made things worse? What then? He wished he understood Maggie's unflagging confidence in his ability to help Mickey.

His hand went automatically to his forehead, where a steady ache pulsed. If only he'd been able to get more than a few hours of restless sleep. But sleep had been an unattainable goal because he'd been haunted by the look of rejection he'd last seen on Maggie's face. And his mind went into guilt mode when he also thought of his years of lying to her.

He knew he should come clean and admit the full truth about what he knew must have looked to Maggie like an unreasonable stand on adoption. But he just couldn't bring himself to tell her that he'd never wanted any children. Theirs or anyone else's.

He still harbored a secret shame because he'd felt only relief when Maggie had been so devastated by the news that she was completely infertile. And now her acceptance of all of the blame for the breakup between them haunted him as well. He had to continue lying to her, but only because he couldn't think of a way to stop without risking everything.

It was the lies, he'd admitted to himself in the dark hours of the night, that kept him from taking the next step toward a complete reconciliation between them. The trouble was that only the lies made reconciliation possible. If she knew the truth about his adoption, she would want nothing to do with him.

It's the only way, he told himself again as the elevator opened on Mickey's floor. He'd have to keep quiet and be the best husband and father he could be. The latter of which might actually be simpler than he'd thought. He was beginning to see that he'd been wrong in his assessment of his ability to love a child. He didn't know about the parenting part yet, but he couldn't imagine loving anyone more than he did his brother's children—and Maggie.

Trent shook his head as he walked absently along, lost in thought. He couldn't risk losing them over a truth Maggie never had to know. There was no reason to open up that Pandora's box and risk everyone's happiness. He just had to get up the courage to risk his heart all the way by moving into the main house—into Maggie's bedroom.

Mickey's therapist had just put him back in bed as Trent entered the room. "Hey, Mick. How was therapy?"

The therapist was a tall African-American woman with the most expressive eyes Trent had ever seen. And those eyes shouted worry. She frowned and glanced down at Mickey. "He has to try harder, Mr. Osborne. I know he could be on his feet right quick if he'd just try."

Mickey crossed his arms and frowned. "I told you! I'm tired. I'm ready for a nap," he muttered.

Trent put his hands on his hips and considered Mickey for a long minute. Mickey squirmed a bit under his scrutiny, giving Trent the hope that his opinion might actually matter to his nephew. "Don't be disrespectful to Ms....?" He raised an enquiring eyebrow toward the therapist.

"Deanna Hart," she replied.

"Don't be disrespectful to Ms. Hart," Trent repeated.

"Sorry," Mickey told the woman, then looked uncertainly back to Trent.

"You know, Mick, I've known you since before you were born. I even bounced you on my knee a time or two at midnight when you were driving your parents crazy because being tired was the last thing you'd admit to. Where do you suppose *that* Mickey's gotten to?" Trent asked Deanna Hart, while pulling on his earlobe in pretended deep thought.

"Can't say, Mr. Osborne."

"Think maybe somebody stole him?" Trent made a grand gesture of checking under the bed. "He's not under here."

"Well, this is the only Mickey Osborne I've ever met. And let me tell you, he's a sleepy little son of a gun. I've got lots of wide-awake patients to see today, so I'd better run along. You give a shout if you get rested up, Mickey Osborne," she called as she sauntered out of the room.

"Mick," Trent said and straddled a chair he'd turned backward. He propped his arm across the back, trying to look relaxed when he was anything but. "That lady does have lots of other patients to see, and very few of them are as lucky as you."

Mickey looked startled. "Lucky?" he all but snarled. "Me?"

"You! Oh, I know what you're thinking—your parents are dead, you're stuck here needing therapy to be able to walk again. But you know what? At least you'll be *able* to walk soon. Many of these kids in here have never walked and never will walk."

"Then why aren't they already in a crippled kids' institution? Or is that what this is?"

"This is a hospital, Mickey. A hospital dedicated to children who need help. I wouldn't call it an institution."

"Then when am I going to the institution?"

Trent frowned. What was going on? Something about this conversation seemed off-kilter. "You're coming home to us as soon as you're well enough."

"No!" Mickey shouted. "I don't want to come home."

Trent felt sweat trickle down his back and pepper his scalp as he grappled to understand what had the boy so upset. "I know it's scary, this new life since the accident. The idea of Aunt Maggie and me being your guardians now must be very hard to grasp along with missing your folks. But we're going to be there for you no matter what. You have to trust us. We love you, Mick.''

"But I *want* to go to the institution. I do. Really!" Mickey cried out. He sounded almost desperate as tears flooded his dark-chocolate-brown eyes.

What bothered Trent about the entire conversation suddenly crystallized. "Mickey, what institution are you talking about? Where did you hear that word? And why would you want to go anywhere besides home."

"Please, Uncle Trent," the boy sobbed. "I know! I know I won't ever get better! I know I'm a burden. I don't want to be. Honest. I know it's a lot of work being our guardian. You sure don't need a crippled kid, too. If I'm not around, it won't be as hard for you and Aunt Maggie to put up with the other kids."

Trent stood and walked in silence to the window. Somebody had been filling this boy's head with a lot of garbage. Stuffing his fisted hands in his pockets, Trent came back to the bed, doing his best to hide his anger. "Mick, I want to know right now where you got these crazy ideas. We don't 'put up' with any of you. We love you. All of you."

Mickey just stared, his eyes confused and tear filled. "I heard them, Uncle Trent. In the hallway. In Florida. They said I would have to go into an institution or be a burden. So I asked some old lady volunteer, and she told me what it meant. I don't want to be a burden," he sobbed. "I don't mind going away."

Trent sat on the edge of the bed and took Mickey's

hands in his. "Mick, son, I don't know who you heard outside your room, but they were dead wrong. You *will* walk again, and I'd never let you go into an institution. Neither would Maggie. Not if we could take care of you properly at home. And you could never be a burden to either of us."

"Yes, I am! Please stay with the other kids and be their daddy. Aunt Maggie just can't do it by herself. Mommy always needed Daddy's help. You got to stay."

His heart stuttered. Words like *institution* and *burden* just weren't in Maggie's vocabulary. Ed would never have presumed to suggest such a thing. Which left only his parents having been at the hospital. And *burden* and *institution* were certainly in *their* vocabulary.

Narrow-eyed, Trent looked down at Mickey. "Did you know the people who you heard talking?"

"They said they were my grandparents, but that their visit was a secret. They didn't stay long, but she said I looked like my daddy. I thought I liked them sort of. At first. But then they said those things outside my room."

"And none of it was true. I want you to believe that. I'm going to tell you a secret, Mick. Your daddy and I are nothing like our parents."

Mickey didn't say anything, but he looked confused "Do you mind the kids?" Mickey ventured, looking up at Trent, hope blazing in his gaze. "They can be noisy."

"I don't care. I love all of you." Trent chuckled, thinking of "noisy," and told Mickey about the excitement his littlest sister had caused the day before. Mickey laughed, and it was the most beautiful sound Trent had ever heard. He found himself wishing Maggie were there to hear it.

Trent was still conflicted with emotions of amazement and anger when he pulled into his parking spot next to the carriage house a few hours later. He felt awe, at what he'd been able to accomplish with Mickey that morning. He'd watched a remarkable change come over the boy and had accompanied him to his second therapy session of the day. A session during which Mickey had made what Deanna Hart had called real progress.

But the anger—lifelong, it felt like—toward his parents roiled deep inside him. Mickey had also overheard a remark about how much more intelligent Trent had always been than Mike. Trent had taken long minutes explaining different talents people have, that they also have different ways of learning, and that his and Mike's parents had never understood that. He tried to paint them not as villains, but as one-dimensional people who didn't understand anyone at all different from themselves.

He found Maggie on the back porch, reading to Daniel and Rachel. He guessed Grace was napping. He checked his watch. This was the time she'd put her down the two previous days. It jolted Trent to realize that they'd only been back from Florida for two days. So much had happened. High on his success, he'd thought as he drove home about moving into the house. But it was too soon—too quick. He had to be sure that it would work between him and Maggie before he trusted her with his heart again.

"How was he?" Maggie asked, as he walked toward her across the yard.

"Good. We had a long talk." He looked significantly toward the two children at her feet. "I'll tell you about it later."

"Rachel, why don't you and Daniel play on the tire swing for a few minutes," Maggie suggested.

Rachel sighed. "I know. Like Grandmom says, 'It's-little-pitchers-have-big-ears time.' Come on, Daniel. I'll push you."

Daniel's voice drifted back at them on the fall breeze. "There's another weird thing big people say. I don't have big ears. And pitchers don't have any ears at all."

Maggie chuckled. "He's so literal. I find myself constantly analyzing every old expression now, just the way he does. So tell me about Mickey. Was he really doing better today, or was that for Rachel and Daniel's benefit?"

Trent smiled and settled in the wicker love seat next to her. "He's doing better. Now." He found it impossible not to reach out and take her hands in his. "You were right. He opened up to me." He squeezed her hands, pure joy bubbling inside him. "I helped him, Mag. Just the way you said I could."

He went on to relay the conversation, and felt a renewal of his anger toward his parents. "I want to go over there and give them both a piece of my mind."

Maggie frowned and shook her head. "Not a good idea. Let's not call attention to ourselves."

"Oh, I won't. But I'd like to."

"I keep hoping that they'll get involved with their lives again and forget about us. I mean, it isn't as if the children, or even you and I, were part of their everyday world."

"That was my take on it, too," Trent said, and let go of one of her hands. He settled back in the love seat but kept her other hand in his grasp, resting their joined hands on his thigh. "Ed's preparing a case even though everything's been quiet."

"That's...that's good." The sudden hesitation in her voice made Trent look up. He hadn't even realized that he'd been stroking the back of her hand with his thumb. Maggie's gaze flicked from their hands to his eyes at the same time. They stared at each other, and he knew that the longing in her gaze had to be in his as well.

Then he looked at her mouth. And nothing on earth could have kept him from leaning forward to cover her lips with his. *It's all still there. Love. Need. Home. You can have it all. Risk it,* his heart urged. He slid his fingers into her hair to cup her head and deepen the kiss. That was when his brain intruded. *She'll leave you one day. No one's ever stayed in your life. No one's ever wanted to. Especially not Maggie.*

The war still waged inside him, but the kiss continued of its own accord until a child's voice broke in. "Yuck! I thought you guys didn't do that kissy stuff with each other." Daniel's disgust changed what could have been an awkward moment into a hilarious

one. Maggie was laughing before their lips even
parted.

"Oh. You just want me to kiss *you?*" Maggie
asked as she pulled Daniel, squirming and shrieking,
onto her lap and kissed him innumerable times anywhere she could. His thick auburn hair felt like silk
as it rubbed against her cheek.

"You're kookoo, Aunt Maggie," Daniel said when
she let him go. He scrambled off her lap and scowled
in an obvious bid to gather his dented four-year-old
dignity. But then he cocked his head to the side and
grinned at her, wrinkling his freckled nose comically,
before turning to run across the yard for his turn on
the tire swing.

Trent was instantly alarmed when Maggie pivoted
toward him with tears forming in her eyes and her
chin quivering. "He laughed," she blurted on a sob.
"I made him laugh."

Self-protection and self-preservation didn't matter
a whit to Trent at that moment. He pulled her into his
arms to comfort her. It was his duty, he told himself,
but with her softness pressed against him, it didn't
feel like duty. It didn't feel like duty when he drew
in her light spring scent or luxuriated in her lush and
silky sable hair, either.

And so he held her. Eyes closed and teeth gritted
against a need for more, he held her until another
intrusion drew his attention.

The crunch of tires in the stone drive and a car
nosing around the side of the house signaled the end
of those precious minutes. Be grateful, he told himself. This is still moving too fast. Feel lucky that

someone else came along. But as he put Maggie away from him and dried her cheeks with his thumbs, he didn't feel grateful or lucky. He felt cheated and lonely.

Their visitor approached carrying Daniel and Rachel who'd run to intercept him. It was Pastor Jim.

"Trent. Maggie. Afternoon. I thought I'd stop by and offer my services. I understand from Sarah's mother and Maggie's that you're working on the old homestead by yourselves. I'm guessing that neither of you knew that I used to help Mike around here. Actually, we traded hours. He lent a hand at The Tabernacle, and I came over here to help out with a lot of the bigger jobs. I'll warn you, though, Harvest Fest is just around the corner. I need help setting up booths."

Trent waited before answering, considering the preacher with a narrow-eyed gaze. Was this just another friend of Mike's offering help, or was it an attempt to lasso him into the church? "I could use a hand, I suppose—and lend one," he agreed, finally. *And* he silently added, *maybe figure out what the attraction is at that church.* After all, if his wife was going to attend church there and take the kids along, he needed to at least understand what was being taught there. And he was ready if the man tried any subtle indoctrination ploys. Besides, he had to admit he was curious, because so far none of the members he'd met seemed the least bit weak or foolish. Which blew his religion theory right out of the water and only heightened his curiosity.

"Would you like to stay for dinner, Pastor Jim?" Maggie asked with a knowing smile.

Jim Dillon laughed, then checked his watch with an expansive gesture. "Well, look at that. It is getting right up there toward dinnertime, isn't it? Don't mind if I do. Thanks, Maggie."

Trent looked from one to the other. "Am I missing something?"

"The women in the congregation, and a few of the men as well, try to keep me fed. My lack of cooking skill is legendary. But it's my only true failing, so don't worry. I'm well-versed in home repair. It was my job before I went into the ministry, and I still earn a little extra money that way."

"Was Mike paying you with more than trading labor?"

"No, I only worked when he did. I guess the next project was the heater tubing. Want to work on that 'til dinner?"

"I warn you, I've only read up on this stuff," Trent said.

"It's easy. We'll have a room ready for the next step by dinner."

Trent was surprised. He seemed to remember several sermons about not working on Sundays. "What about all that not-working-on-the-Sabbath doctrine?"

"Jesus came to free us from the law, not reinforce it. We're free to do what has to be done. That's why he cured the blind man on the Sabbath. To show us that if what we do glorifies God, then there's nothing wrong with it. And besides that, this is fun for me. Not really work at all. How about you?"

Trent grinned, realizing that it was indeed fun, and not just a duty he was left to fulfill for Mike. Lately, he'd certainly come to enjoy working with his hands more than he did working at his own company with computer software. Dealing with anything at CSD left him flat. Maybe he should seriously entertain some of the buyout offers that he was always getting. "Yeah, Pastor, actually it is fun. Maybe because I was never allowed to get dirty as a kid."

Jim laughed. "Well, then. Let's go have some fun and see if we can't get you a little dirty. And could we dispense with the 'Pastor' stuff? It makes me feel old, and I think I'm a couple years younger than you."

Three weeks later Trent hooked up the last of the piping, making all the rooms ready for heat. And it was just in time. Fall had settled in, and he was close to considering Jim Dillon a friend. Jim had answered a few of Trent's idle questions about faith and about the Bible, but not once had he pressured Trent to attend his church. And Trent was more confused than ever about religion.

He'd managed to keep busy enough these last weeks that being close to Maggie hadn't become a problem again, but as he'd learned already, this kind of work often left his brain free to think. And he usually found himself pondering his life. Lately his thoughts centered on Maggie.

He'd learned something stunning about her, and wondered if it had anything to do with her new faith. She was not the same woman who'd left him after ten years of marriage. She had an uncanny ability to roll with the punches now. She took Grace's decorating the bathroom rug with toothpaste in stride. Hadn't even flinched when Grace had decorated her still baby-round tummy in the same vein but with indelible marker. She'd actually laughed last night when Daniel, with Rachel's help, had practiced his Noah costume for the Harvest Fest by slicking his auburn hair back with a gooey mixture of petroleum jelly sprinkled liberally with baby powder. Nothing flustered her where the children were concerned.

Mickey was fighting back now and was well on the way to full recovery. He was due home in a few days, and though he still needed physical therapy and used a walker, he would return to school soon as well. The children's grief was lessening, and with each passing day they were better able to talk about Mike and Sarah, remembering happy times with their parents in a true spirit of joy. Trent hadn't realized how resilient children were.

As he walked up the steps from the basement, Maggie came into the kitchen—he couldn't believe how bad his timing was. His love for her was like a caged thing, clawing at him to be set free. But he kept those feelings locked up and out of sight. He wanted to trust her, but every time he tried to reach out, his mind snared his heart and held it back, keeping the impulse in check.

"So that *was* you I heard down here. All the children are upstairs. You were the only one I could think of, but I couldn't imagine that you'd be at it already," Maggie said.

"I wanted to get an early start on the heater. Jim's coming over this afternoon. We're going to fire up the system and see what we get."

"Heat, I hope. It got a little chilly last night. I was up three or four times, checking to make sure everybody had stayed covered. Of course, they hadn't."

Trent forced himself to look into her eyes for the first time in three weeks. She looked so tired and drawn this morning, and there were dark smudges beneath her doe eyes. *I should be here to take some of the middle-of-the-night burden.*

Now guilt assailed him. He supposed the children often caused her to lose sleep during the night. The first night after the accident, Rachel had kept Maggie up all night with nightmares. He frowned. When he'd explained that he would be using the carriage house, he'd told her to call him if she needed him, but now he realized Maggie would never do that. Looking into her tired eyes was like staring the truth in the face. This situation between them couldn't go on much longer this way. He missed her. And he knew she missed him.

Rachel skipped into the kitchen just then, breaking the connection between them. She stopped short and her smile faded, her brown eyes going suddenly grave when she looked at Trent. "Oh, you're working again this Sunday morning." Her disappointment was palpable.

"I only have a little time each night and on the weekends, and there's an awful lot left to finish on the house. I have to get this heat going today, sweetheart. We had frost last night."

"But can't you do it later? You never come to church with us."

Daniel came in just then and added his two cents. "Daddy said work can always wait, but God shouldn't have to 'cause he does so much for us. We want you to come with us."

Trent could have debated Mike's axiom all day, but it was important to preserve his brother's memory in a positive way for his children. "I'm not dressed for church, kids," he said instead, and checked his watch. "And you have to get on the road in less than an hour."

"A lot of guys go dressed like that," Daniel protested. "Pastor Jim always wears jeans."

"I've been working in these clothes," Trent said, beginning to feel trapped.

Intellectually he knew that was foolish. Just because he drove his family to church didn't mean he had to subscribe to the whole religious nine yards. It was good for kids to go to church—to have that strong moral grounding, he reminded himself. If he insisted on staying home, someday they might balk at going.

So he'd go. He didn't have to go, he assured himself. But he'd go.

"Okay," he said, trying to sound cheerful and not as if he were on the way to the dentist. "I'll go wash up and change. It won't take long. I can always grab something and eat it on the way. Be back as soon as I can."

He was halfway across the porch when he realized his error. Until then he'd managed to keep his residence in the carriage house a secret. He held his breath, hoping the kids didn't notice, but then Daniel's voice drifted out the door.

"Why's Uncle Trent going to the workshop to change?"

Chapter Ten

Maggie saw Trent halt midstep. Good. He'd heard
Daniel's question. She wondered what his answer
would be, or if he'd leave her to answer it herself.
She'd been waiting for both these explosive questions, and it struck her as rather humorous that both
had come in the same conversation.

Trent pivoted, looking dismayed.

On the hot seat for the second time in only minutes.

Maggie settled back to enjoy herself, but stood by,
her hands on Rachel's shoulders, ready to help out—
for Trent's sake as well as the children's. She knew
she'd enjoy seeing him squirm, but she didn't want
him to fall flat on his face.

"Come here, partner," Trent said, then directed
Daniel over to the wicker settee. After lifting the four-
year-old onto his knee, Trent appeared more com-
posed. "Do you remember that Aunt Maggie and I

weren't living together before we moved here to take care of you and your brother and sisters?''

Daniel nodded. ''Uh-huh.''

''It takes time for adults to get used to living in the same house. Like…can you sort of remember the way you had to get used to having Baby Grace around?''

Head bobbing in agreement, Daniel replied, ''Mommy said I kept waking her up 'cause it was okay to yell before, so I kept forgetting.''

''Exactly. And believe me, it's even harder for one adult to get used to living with another adult. Which gets us back to Aunt Maggie and me. I didn't want us to get in each other's way or to get on each other's nerves. So I gave us both a little space of our own for a while 'til we get used to each other again. Sort of *half* moving in together. I've been spending the nights after all you kids go to bed in the apartment over the workshop.''

Daniel grinned. ''Wow. You get to sleep in the carriage house? That's cool! Can I come stay with you when Rachel gets in my way?''

''You have your own room to go to when you need time alone. I'd share one with Aunt Maggie if I stayed in the house. See the difference?'' Daniel nodded, but was obviously disappointed. Trent looked up at Maggie with a triumphant grin as if to say, *See? problem solved.*

''Uncle Trent, where are your nerves? How do people get on them?'' Daniel enquired. His brown eyes, wide and fringed with long curling lashes, looked endearingly innocent.

The look on Trent's face was priceless in contrast,

and had just the right tinge of horror to tickle Maggie's funny bone. She grinned and said, "He's all yours, oh, wise one. Come on, Rachel, let's go get your hair fixed and wake Grace, while Uncle Trent explains this one."

Of course, that look was nothing to his expression later in the afternoon when Daniel started explaining to Pastor Dillon that Trent slept in the carriage house because Aunt Maggie got on Uncle Trent's nerves. Maggie was only too glad to leave Trent to do his explaining alone once again.

She knew she shouldn't revel in his discomfort, and should probably be just as embarrassed as he was to have the intimate details of their lives revealed to her pastor. But she wasn't. Not just because she had already discussed her marriage in detail with Jim Dillon, but because there *were* no intimate details. None whatsoever. And that was no one's fault but Trent's. She had every confidence that her pastor and friend would instinctively know that.

Since that Sunday afternoon three weeks earlier when Trent had kissed her with such passion then later held her when she'd cried, he'd been standoffish and distant. It hurt, because during those few shining moments he'd made her believe that he still cared.

Then he'd withdrawn into a familiar pattern. He was unreachable beneath a shell of activity and overwork. He was "keeping too busy to think." It was so typical that it would have been funny had it not been so sad. It was classic Trent Osborne, with a new wrinkle. Maggie didn't think she was being paranoid in believing that he actually fled every time they wound up alone together.

She understood that she'd hurt him in the past. She understood that he was afraid to be hurt again. But what she didn't understand was how she was supposed to convince him that she'd never hurt him like that again if he wouldn't even spend five minutes alone in the same room with her.

Each night Maggie emerged from Grace's room, hoping to find him waiting for her somewhere in the house. He was never there. It wasn't as if he was necessary to her survival. She was getting along all right and adjusting to her new life, because she had the comfort of her faith. But she still needed Trent's love. She needed to share her thoughts with him. She needed him to hold her when she was worried or sad. She needed the joy and excitement of being in his arms throughout the long nights.

Shaking her head to drive off thoughts of what was wrong with her life, Maggie forced herself to focus on what was right with it. She had Trent back, and all the time in the world to prove her love to him. She had the children, who, though it took a lot of time and energy to care for them, were worth every second's effort.

Maggie didn't know why she'd let herself get mired in negative thoughts, but figured it had something to do with how tired she felt today. The room even tilted a bit when she turned toward the back door as it opened.

''I'm going to have to pull up the corner of the boy's bathroom to fix that leak on the family room ceiling,'' Trent said as he came in carrying a tote full of tools.

Maggie checked the clock. An hour 'til bedtime for the children. She sighed. Why was she so tired? ''Does that mean you're going to turn off the water? I was going to do a couple of loads of laundry.''

''Not yet. I have to tear up the floor first. You could probably get a load done before I'm ready.''

''Okay, don't forget bedtime for this crew is in an hour.''

Trent nodded. ''I'll have the noisy part done by then.''

''I'll get the wash started right away,'' she told him, and they went their separate ways—he upstairs and she to the laundry room in the basement.

Forty-five minutes later the banging stopped, and she heard the *whir* of a power drill floating down the back stairs. Maggie's first load of laundry was ready to go in the dryer, so she trudged back down the basement stairs. The *whir* was now overpowered by a rough grinding sound. Halfway across the basement, she was suddenly deluged: cold water, and over a hundred years' worth of accumulated dust and dirt poured down on her head. All her brain functions just stopped. She stood there stupefied.

Footsteps thundered down the rickety wooden steps toward her, but it was only when she saw the look of utter horror on Trent's face that the log jam in her brain broke. Laughter welled up inside her and erupted.

''Maggie, you're all wet!'' he shouted over her uncontrolled hysterics and the rushing sound of the indoor waterfall.

Pushing her sopping hair out of her eyes, Maggie nodded and tripped forward out of the flow. "Yeah. Wet's definitely what I am." She gestured toward the gushing water. "Maybe you should turn it off."

"Off! Right!" he agreed, and rushed to the main shut-off valve. The stream turned instantly to a trickle, then intermittent drips. "I can't believe I did that." He grabbed an old blanket and tossed it over her shoulders, then started rubbing her arms. "I feel so stupid!"

"What did you do?"

"Jim told me to drill a little pilot hole in the subflooring, then tap with a pencil to make sure the pipe wasn't right under the drill before I used the hole cutter."

"Then how did you hit a pipe?" She gestured to the ceiling. "I'm assuming you hit a pipe."

"I feel so stupid," Trent said again. "I just didn't think."

"Didn't th-think w-what?" she asked, suddenly quaking with cold chills.

"About the eraser. I used the eraser end of the pencil. No wonder I didn't hear it hit the pipe. I'm so sorry, Maggie. I'll have it fixed as soon as I can. But let's get you in a hot shower to warm you up first. You're shivering."

She chuckled. "C-can't. You j-just t-turned off all the wa-water."

"That bathroom has separate valves. I'll get them now and isolate the boys' bath from the rest of the house. Then we'll get you warmed up in that hot shower.''

Trent hurried to restore the main water supply.

''There we go. All secure,'' he told her when he returned to where she still stood shivering.

Oddly, cold as she was, Maggie hadn't yet been able to get up the energy to climb the stairs so she could take off her wet clothes. Her head ached and her limbs felt as heavy as lead. Her bedroom seemed so far away.

''Now, Maggie, let's get you warmed up,'' Trent said, steering her toward the steps. Maggie staggered as she shuffled along, trying to keep the cold cloth from connecting any more than was necessary. Before she knew what he intended, Trent had scooped her into his arms and was carrying her upstairs.

''I'll get you all wet,'' she protested.

Trent chuckled. ''Mag, sweetie, I'm the one who got you all wet, remember?''

''Oh,'' she said dreamily. Feeling a little like Scarlett O'Hara, Maggie decided it was worth an icy drenching to feel his arms around her—to have him behave so gallantly toward her. Then she tried to admonish herself. *Where's your pride? Your self-respect?*

Pride and self-respect don't make you feel what being in his arms does, another voice called out from the depths of her being. And Maggie listened to that voice. She dropped her head on Trent's broad shoulder and just breathed in the beloved scent of the man she'd love 'til the day she died.

''What happened?'' Rachel asked when they got to

the top of the steps. Her big brown eyes were wide as saucers.

"A pipe sprayed cold water everywhere."

Rachel stared at them. "All over Aunt Maggie, too?"

Trent grimaced. "She...sort of got in the way of the flood. She needs a warm shower and dry clothes. Do me a favor, Rach. Put a video in for your brother and sister, and keep an eye on them for a little while longer. I'll be right back down."

Maggie didn't protest. She didn't have the energy. And her chest felt suddenly heavy. Her head didn't feel any better, either. Trent adjusted the shower and helped her undress. Then, after checking on the children, he returned to help her dry off and dress in a warm flannel gown. She wished she wasn't so tired because she scarcely had the energy to enjoy all the loving attention.

"You need to be in bed, Mag. I'll tuck the kids in, then come back to help you dry your hair. Maybe you can get a little sleep in the meantime."

Maggie nodded meekly and sank down on the bed, grateful for its softness. Trent frowned down at her, his eyebrows nearly meeting in the middle. He put his hand on her forehead. "You're all flushed, and you feel warm, too."

"I'm just tired. Really. Thanks for this. I don't think I could do bedtime tonight."

"Don't worry about it. I'll handle it."

"Grace sometimes likes to be rocked for a few minutes after the other two have calmed down."

"Maggie, I'll handle it. You rest. And, sweetheart, I'm sorry about the water."

"'s okay," she muttered and sniffled, praying he'd leave before she lost the battle with the ridiculous tears dammed at the back of her throat. Just when she'd gotten good and mad at him for ignoring her, he had to turn around and be sweet and gentle and solicitous. The man didn't play fair!

The tears never had a chance because Maggie drifted off before Trent left the room. Before she knew it, though, he returned, and stuffed extra pillows behind her back. Then he started drying her hair with the hair dryer. All she could do was watch the play of undecipherable emotion move across his face, and stare into his beautiful blue eyes as he ran a brush through her hair.

It was all so wonderful. Like a dream. Then a horrifying thought occurred to her. *No, Lord,* she prayed. *Don't let me be sick. Who will take care of the children? Who will finish the wash? I can't get sick. If I leave Trent with all this responsibility, how will he stand it? He doesn't have You. He doesn't know how hard this is. And he didn't want all this responsibility in the first place.*

"I promise not to be sick," she told Trent. He leaned forward as if to hear her, and she caught the scent of him once again. She reached up to stroke his jaw. It was rough and scratchy with a day's beard growth, but it felt wonderful to Maggie. It felt like old times. She closed her eyes and sighed. "I'm not sick. Can't be," she muttered.

She heard his, "Oh, yes, you can be, love," reply,

but it just sort of floated over her head and made no sense. She looked up into Trent's concerned face and dismissed his words. She never got sick.

She didn't bother to protest, though. What he said didn't matter anyway, because Maggie felt as if she were wrapped in a warm cocoon. As if she were seeing everything from behind a dark, silken veil. The world had become muzzy, muted and cloudy. It was lovely.

Maggie numbly swallowed aspirin with juice, just the way he ordered, then she smiled up at him. But he didn't smile back. He only frowned and stuck a thermometer in her mouth. After that, everything faded except a lot of strange aches and pains then even they began to dim.

One conscious thought stayed with her as she slept. Even deep behind the insulating veil, she felt Trent's presence. This time he didn't leave her alone in the night.

Chapter Eleven

Trent stood at the window staring out at the night and remembered the last few hours....

He had been at his wit's end, sitting in a rocking chair in the nursery with Grace screaming on his knee. Even Rachel and Daniel's attempts to distract her from Maggie's absence hadn't worked. Then Rachel had flopped at his feet, exhausted. "I wish the house was a car, Uncle Trent," she'd said. "She always falls asleep when she's in the car and she's tired."

A few minutes later turning the corner from Newtown Road onto Sugartown Road, Trent smiled and sighed at the blessed quiet that had settled. He made one left, then another when he came to the drive of Paradise Found. Now all he had to do was get them all in the house and into bed without waking Grace.

After accomplishing that seemingly impossible task, Trent went to check on Maggie and to give her some aspirin and juice. Earlier she'd protested that she was only tired, but Trent was sure she was sick. He'd hated leaving her alone in the house, but he'd had to get Grace to sleep so Rachel and Daniel, who both had school in the morning, could get to sleep at a decent hour.

Maggie was still sleeping soundly, so he set the thermometer, juice and bottle of aspirin on the night table. He hated to wake her, but she needed something to bring that fever down, and he didn't think it was a good idea to let her hair air dry. While standing next to the bed for a minute, Trent drank in her sweet face. She looked almost peaceful except for a little crease between her eyebrows that told him she was in some sort of pain. Her cheeks were still flushed, too, and the rest of her face was pale. When he laid his hand across her forehead, he found more heat than before.

After locating her hair dryer and brush, Trent woke Maggie. She opened her eyes and stared up at him. He didn't trust himself to speak, but set to work. *I miss you,* he longed to confess, but just went on drying her rich, shining hair.

Her eyes widened in obvious dismay just as he turned off the dryer. "I promise not to be sick," she whispered. Her voice was so low that he had to lean forward just to hear her. He wasn't prepared for her touch or the feelings it evoked when she reached up and rubbed her palm across his cheek. She closed her eyes and a quiet moan whooshed into the room. "I'm not sick. Can't be," he heard her pledge.

Trent turned his face and kissed her palm. "Oh,

yes, you can be, love," he told her. It struck him in that instant what a fool he'd been. Why had he been so determined to keep at arm's length the one person who had ever made him feel whole? And loved.

He wasn't protecting himself emotionally. He was punishing her. She'd begged, really begged, for his forgiveness. And now, looking down at her beloved, pale face, he was ashamed that he'd withheld that forgiveness for so long. She, too, had been hurt, and her leaving had been at least partially his fault.

"Here, Maggie honey, time for some juice and aspirin," he told her as he lifted her hand and put the tablets in her palm. She looked up at him with fevered eyes and obediently took the pills. Her dreamy smile disappeared when he held out the thermometer, but she let him tuck it under her tongue. She continued to watch him with glassy brown eyes that gradually went less and less focused, then closed...

He'd read the thermometer and had rushed to the phone. His Maggie had needed more than aspirin: she'd needed a doctor and he had been bound and determined to get one to come to her. He occasionally played handball with a doctor at his health club, and in minutes had managed to cajole Dr. Jerry Wilson into coming out to the house.

A few hours later, after thanking Jim Dillon for picking up the prescription Wilson had called in, Trent settled carefully into bed next to Maggie. He didn't want to wake her. She needed her sleep and time to heal. When she turned toward him and snuggled close, Trent was glad of his decision to change things between them from that night forward. He closed his eyes and let the glorious feeling of holding her close flow through him.

It was joy.

It was agony.

It was a long time before he slept.

The electronic *buzz* of Maggie's alarm catapulted Trent out of bed at seven the next morning. His heart pounding, he sank back down. He hated alarm clocks. He preferred to wake to music, or at least to the patter of the traffic-watch chopper pilots. Maggie, on the other hand, slept through anything except the distinctive *buzz* of an alarm clock. They'd compromised on a clock radio during their marriage, and he'd had the pleasure of waking her for nine years, eleven months and twelve days.

Trent twisted in bed and his eyes came to rest on Maggie. And now he'd have that pleasure again. But not today. She was paler this morning, though her cheeks were flushed. He reached across the bed and touched her forehead with the back of his hand. Trent frowned. She was still overly warm.

Maggie's eyelashes fluttered, then rose to reveal her fevered brown eyes. "You stayed."

The awe in her voice shamed him. "I couldn't leave you so sick, sweetheart. Do you remember Jerry Wilson being here?"

"Your handball partner? No. Why was he here?"

Trent smiled at her confusion. "Because he's a doctor and you needed one."

"Oh. I... You went to so much trouble." She

licked her dry lips, and Trent remembered Jerry's orders about drinking plenty of liquids.

"I'll get you some water," he said, then went to the bathroom to fetch it. He returned and was shocked to see tears in her eyes. "Are you feeling worse?"

Maggie shook her head and bit her lip as her tears welled up even more, then flowed from the corner of her eyes into her hair. Her heavy eyes drifted shut then, and he never found out the cause of her tears, but he was very much afraid that in some way he was responsible.

Trent got Rachel and Daniel off to school, then fed and dressed Grace. He'd just gotten off the phone with Ester, who reported that she and Nancy were both down with the same bug. What was he going to do about his afternoon meeting with the president of the conglomerate interested in buying CSD? It was only an exploratory meeting but it wasn't a meeting he wanted to postpone. Trent saw no other option. He'd just lifted the receiver to call Ellen, his secretary, to have her call off the meeting, when a knock came at the back door.

It was Jim Dillon with an elderly woman. "How's Maggie this morning?" the pastor asked.

"A little better, but not much," Trent answered as he stepped back and gestured to them to come in. "She woke up long enough to have some juice at least. She's still pretty sick. Can I get either of you some coffee? I just made a pot."

"Goodness, no," the round little woman with the graying hair exclaimed. "You have enough on your plate without having to wait on us. How are you doing, Trent?'' she asked, and stuck out her hand.

Bemused, Trent shook it. ''I'm fine. Have we met?'' he said, searching his memory for a name.

''Claire White. We met briefly at the memorial service.''

''I'm sorry I—''

''Relax, young man,'' Mrs. White cut in, then laughed. It was a musical sound that had a young, carefree ring to it that surprised Trent. ''No one expects you to remember the people you met that morning. I work in the church nursery with the two-year-olds. I know Grace quite well, and even Daniel and Rachel since they went through my nursery themselves. I also sat for Sarah and Mike on a regular basis. When I heard how burdened you are with Maggie so ill, I asked Pastor Dillon to bring me right on over. So…you get yourself ready for work, and I'll just go on into the family room and see my little dears.''

''I got Rachel and Daniel off to school. It's only Grace, and I got out her old playpen to keep her safe while I got the rest of the house under control. I don't know how Maggie does all this. Daniel's due home at twelve-thirty. The nursery school van brings him up the drive.''

Mrs. White patted his hand and nodded, then she took herself off to see Grace. Trent just watched her go in amazement.

''Close your mouth, my friend. There really are people in the world you can count on. And The Tabernacle just happens to lay claim to several of them.

I have some dinners in the car that have to be refrigerated. Can you help me in with them before you get ready for work? And, Trent, you can count on the Lord even more than you can His church.''

Trent nodded, not trusting the steadiness of his voice. When Jim was several yards in front of him on their trek across the lawn, Trent cleared his throat to rid it of a burning sensation that felt embarrassingly like the beginnings of tears. He wondered if Jim really knew something that he didn't. He'd never been able to count on anyone. Even Maggie's love had eventually failed him. It would be nice to have someone to lean on. There was no denying that.

He tucked the thought inside his head for later consideration, and followed Jim to the van. They transferred enough dinners for a week to the freezer and refrigerator, then Jim left.

Even with Mrs. White there, Trent was worried about leaving. But he couldn't put off the meeting. He'd had many other offers for the company over the past few years, but for the first time he found himself seriously considering selling. And that was because the company was no longer as important to him as it had once been. Time with Maggie and the children had supplanted CSD in his mind and heart.

It was a good offer, Trent thought several hours later as he pulled the car around behind the house. One he just might take. And the best part was that for the first time, the buyer hadn't tried to tie him to the company's future. If he sold out, he didn't want to stay on, take orders and watch others make decisions about the company he'd built from scratch.

Mrs. White smiled up at him as he opened the kitchen door. "My, you're home early," she said. "Grace is down for a nap, and Rachel and Daniel are out at their playhouse. As near as I can tell, Maggie slept the whole time you've been gone. I fixed her some broth and tea. I was about to take it up to her but since you're here, you can take it for me. That way you can check on her yourself and say hello."

Trent didn't waste any time. He found Maggie on her way back from the bathroom. She looked weak and unsteady on her feet. Quickly he put the tray on the dresser and rushed to her side. "You shouldn't be out of bed," he said, and scooped her into his arms.

"This is getting to be a habit," she said, and grinned wanly.

"Complaining?"

"Not me. I always envied Scarlett O'Hara."

"I didn't envy Rhett. I had you."

"I'm sorry I left," she said, as he put her down on the bed.

Trent didn't say anything. He covered her with the sheet and blanket, then sat on the bed next to her. "And I'm sorry I didn't forgive you the first time you said that. I've wasted a lot of precious time."

Maggie's eyes widened and tears instantly glistened in their mahogany depths. "You mean that? You forgive me?"

"As if it never happened, sweetheart. I was so worried about you last night, and it made me see how stupid it was to go on the way we were. And how stupid I was to continue to deny my feelings and to keep you at arm's length. I miss you, Mag.'' He pulled her against his chest and nestled her head beneath his chin. He just held her, absorbing her softness, her nearness, for a long time. It wasn't enough, but it would have to do for now. Because even as he wished for more, he had only to feel the heat of her fevered skin to remember that she was ill.

"Come on, sweet Maggie,'' he said, finally managing to break away. "Let's get some of this broth and tea into you. Mrs. White's probably as good a cook as she is a baby-sitter.''

Bedtime that night, after Mrs. White was long gone, was a repeat of the night before. Except that the ruckus started downstairs in the family room. Not wanting Maggie to be disturbed, Trent hurried the kids out to the car again. And once again, Grace fell asleep, but it took half an hour of driving the twisting roads of their little county before she did.

He was in the middle of congratulating himself when a bar of flashing red-and-blue lights came up behind him. Trent pulled over, thinking the policeman wanted to pass him on the narrow country road. But the police cruiser pulled in behind the van. After a few minutes the officer got out and approached.

"What's the trouble, Officer?'' Trent whispered, hoping against hope that all his driving wasn't about to be undone.

"Sir, could I see—''

"Shh. Keep your voice down. You'll wake them.''

"I'd like to see your license and registration," the officer said, not lowering his voice even an octave.

"Okay, but keep your voice down. I have to get back to the house before my wife needs me. She's sick." Trent handed over the pertinent information, and the officer gave him a cool stare. "Did I run a stop sign or something?"

"We've had—"

"Keep your voice down. Please. I have to get these kids in bed before Maggie needs her medicine."

The officer flicked a flashlight into the back of the van, and Trent held his breath. But the light didn't wake the children. "What are you doing driving around and around with a car full of kids? We've had complaints from two of the estates around here that someone is casing the neighborhood in a van. This van."

"Casing the neighborhood? I'm trying to get my kids to sleep without disturbing my sick wife." Had he just said *his* kids? Trent was so astonished at his slip of the tongue that he missed what the officer said next. "Excuse me?"

"I said," the officer whispered, "at first I thought you had a screw loose. Now I *know* you do."

Trent smiled, lighthearted suddenly. "Yeah. But what a way to go. I have another one who's eight years old, but he's in the hospital. You'd be surprised how much fun kids are. Can I go put them to bed now?"

He handed Trent his license and registration. "Yeah, but if you're going to do this tomorrow night," he grumbled, "vary your route a little. Please."

Trent drove home, chuckling to himself all the way. He'd told the truth. The kids were a lot more fun than trouble. What was that old slogan? *You've come a long way, baby.*

It took a week for Maggie to recover completely, but that first twenty-four hours was long enough to open Trent's eyes and load on the guilt. She'd needed help with these kids when he wasn't there or when he was tied up with the renovations. If she'd had it, she might never have become ill in the first place.

Now he had to tell her what he'd done, he thought as he trudged up the stairs to the second floor. He wasn't looking forward to this.

He found Maggie standing in the doorway to the laundry room that he'd finished that afternoon. The sun shone in the window at the back of the narrow room and right through her sable hair, highlighting it with a tinge of red. Today was her first full day out of bed. He hoped she wasn't too tired now that it was bedtime, and he hoped his news didn't annoy her because he desperately wanted to take their renewed relationship one final step further. It was almost all he could think about.

And the waiting was killing him.

Trent wrapped his arms around Maggie's small waist and rested his head atop hers. "Are you standing here awed and amazed, or did I arrange it all wrong?" he asked her.

Maggie shook her head and looked back up at him

over her shoulder, a smile lighting her face. "It's perfect."

"Good," he said, and trailed his hand up her back to rest on her shoulder. "I'll tell Claire you like it. She helped me with the design. Or you can...tell her tomorrow yourself."

Maggie nodded, and turned slightly to face him. She looked a little puzzled. "I'll give her a call in the morning."

"You, uh...won't need to. She'll be here."

"Trent, I'm fine now," Maggie protested, and gave the hand he'd rested on her shoulder a little squeeze.

"You're fine now. But you weren't. It's my fault you—"

"I didn't get sick because of getting wet!"

Trent shrugged and dropped his hand. "Who knows why you got sick? The point is that you *did* get sick. Your reserves were low. No one else caught what your mother and Nancy had except you." He took a deep breath. "Mag, I offered Claire White a job helping you with the kids and the light housework."

Maggie stared at him. She didn't look mad. Just surprised. "Claire? Why on earth would you do that? And without asking me?"

"Because I was afraid you'd say no, and I know this is the best thing for all of us. You agreed in principle weeks ago to hiring someone to help out, but when you got back from Florida you never did anything about it."

"I didn't want a stranger here when we were all trying to feel our way through all the changes."

"Claire isn't a stranger to the kids. They're crazy about her."

"But it's such an imposition on her. She volunteers at the church all the time—and do you know she lives with her son and daughter-in-law? They might not like her working."

"Did *you* know that she misses having kids around now that her grandchildren are in college?" he countered with a smile. He'd missed trying to outwit Maggie. "Or that she's getting tired of her son telling her what to do all the time? We'd be helping her."

Maggie frowned, no doubt seeing her side of the discussion floundering. "No. I had no idea about any of that. But she lives about fifteen miles away. Does she even drive?"

"No, she doesn't drive. That's why I offered her the apartment over the carriage house to live in. It's unoccupied now. She said she misses having a place of her own. And I offered to take her home to her son's on the weekends if she wants to go. She's thrilled with the whole arrangement. I hope you will be. She won't accept until she talks to you. Jim Dillon is bringing her over again in the morning."

At last, Maggie smiled again. "The kids all love her already. I think she'll be a lot of help. Thanks, Trent. This is a great idea."

"I had another idea," he said as he reached out and wrapped his arms around her. A pang of conscience hit him, almost dissuading him from taking the next step. He should tell her about his lie. He should tell her their breakup hadn't been all her fault. But he silenced that inner voice. She never had to know. There was no reason to dredge up all that pain. To admit to a flaw he had yet to identify himself.

Maggie looked up at him, startled. Unsure. "What?"

Trent pushed ahead. They could not go on as they had been—*he* could not. "I locked up downstairs. I thought we'd turn in early."

Maggie nodded, her eyes suddenly alert.

"You need to keep your strength up."

"Oh," she said, her voice flat and heavy with disappointment.

And Trent rejoiced inwardly. He cupped her face in his hands and lowered his head toward hers, watching her reaction. The desire glittering in her eyes before she closed them was everything he'd hoped for. His lips met hers, and he closed his eyes to lose himself in a long, lingering, deeply satisfying kiss. Yes. This was right.

"And I'll make sure that you sleep late tomorrow," he told her, his lips grazing hers with each whispered word.

"Oh," she said, and this time the simple sound had the ring of joy.

Chapter Twelve

A loud *bang* blasted Maggie into consciousness the
next morning. That she was still in Trent's arms was
the first coherent thought she had. Her second was
that either they had both slept through the alarm, or
they hadn't remembered to set it in the first place.
Maggie grinned. Her mind had certainly been else-
where, and as she recalled, so had Trent's.

Grace's crib banged again against the wall in the
room adjoining the master suite. This time she chuckled. Their littlest human alarm clock was in fine form.

Trent groaned. "It can't be morning. Do you think
you could get her to believe it's not morning yet?"

Maggie rolled to her back as Trent propped himself
up on his elbow. She smiled as she looked up into
his sleepy eyes and ran her hand along his beard-
roughened jaw. "Not a chance. I've learned that you
don't reason about bed with a two-year-old. Besides,
in about two more minutes the others will be awake,

too. She yawned. "What time is it anyway? Don't you have to get ready for work?"

Trent grimaced. "It's seven-fifteen, and yes, I do. I have a nine o'clock meeting that I just can't postpone."

"If you have to be downtown at nine, I'd better get breakfast started. Suppose I make pancakes?" Maggie asked.

"That's too much trouble."

"No, it isn't." She laughed as she slipped out of his arms and out of bed. "After all," she added, walking away, "you have to keep up your strength." She stopped in the doorway and winked at him over her shoulder just as she pushed the bathroom door closed behind her.

Trent's laughter followed her, wrapped its arms around her, and danced up her spine.

Maggie poured the last of the batter on the griddle just as Trent came down the back stairs into the kitchen. He was dressed for his meeting except for the suit jacket he had slung over his shoulder. "Good morning, everyone," he said, grinning hugely. He had the look of a very happy man.

After hooking the jacket over his chair, Trent came back to stand behind Maggie at the stove. He kissed her on the back of the neck and wound his arms about her waist. "And a special good morning to my lovely wife."

Maggie laughed. "Flattery like that will get you—" she looked over at their enraptured audience "—um...pancakes!"

Trent raised an eyebrow. "Pancakes? You already promised me that," he teasingly reminded her before letting her go. But he didn't go far. He leaned back against the countertop next to the stove and fiddled with her hair. "How about company for lunch? Just you and me. Claire should be here by then to watch the kids. I thought maybe we'd go to the General Warren Inn. I can probably pick you up by one. How's that sound?"

Tipping her head to the side, she stared at him. Years ago he used to spring surprise lunches like this on her. This was a wonderful blast from the past. She thought about the candlelit atmosphere at the colonial inn and said dreamily, "The General Warren. It sounds...romantic."

Trent grinned. "Count on it." He kissed the tip of her nose.

Daniel's tapping of his blunt fingertips on the table drew their attention. He stared over at them, a thoughtful expression in his brown eyes, his chin propped on the heel of his other hand. "I guess Aunt Maggie isn't getting on your nerves anymore," he said with great disgust.

Maggie and Trent both turned, each of them battling laughter while ostensibly looking for something in the refrigerator. Trent grumbled, "So much for romance" under his breath, and almost undid Maggie's efforts.

She took a deep breath and went up on tiptoe to kiss him. "Michael and Sarah must have found a way for romantic moments," she whispered. "We will, too."

"And we'll start with lunch?" he asked.

Maggie nodded. "Lunch," she promised, then sought a safer subject. "So tell me what this morning's meeting is all about."

Maggie finished with her mascara and picked up her blush brush. She'd had an interesting morning. It had followed one of the most wonderful nights of her life. Trent's sudden return to her arms last night had been an incredible shock. But his revelation over breakfast had left her flabbergasted. He was seriously considering selling CSD! While she had longed for children, CSD had been his baby. And his reason for the sale—that he wanted more time with her and the children—had left her dazed. Happily dazed, she thought as she stared at her reflection.

Thank you, Lord. You really are the great author and finisher. You've taken a tragedy none of us knew how we'd get through and turned it into something wonderful.

Just how much of a miracle had come about was never more evident than when Jim Dillon came by with Claire and her belongings just after Trent left for the city. He and Maggie had talked about Trent for a while. Apparently, the young pastor confided, the Lord was often the main topic of conversation when he and Trent were alone. Maggie couldn't help but be encouraged that Trent was questioning his skewed view of faith. He was seeking the Lord even if he was unaware of it.

Seven weeks later, before he sat down to the Thanksgiving table, Trent looked around at everyone as they all scrambled for seats. Sometimes when he thought of the changes these last months had wrought, it seemed unreal to him. Wonderfully unreal and horribly frightening. What if all this disappeared? He couldn't go back. He knew that. Not now. Not after he'd finally begun to live the life he and Maggie had started out wanting all those years ago when they'd taken their wedding vows.

He glanced at Maggie as she buckled Grace into her high chair, and guilt crept in to steal even more of his happiness. It killed him a little more every time her eyes clouded whenever anyone mentioned something that had happened during the period of their separation. He wished he could bring himself to tell her the truth. He should have told her in Florida. He should have put aside his hurt and eased her guilt as much as he could. And now it was too late. Because as much as he wanted to tell her, he was so afraid of losing her that he was paralyzed.

"Suppose we each tell the Lord what we're thankful for today," Maggie said as she sat. Her voice drew Trent from his thoughts. *Pray out loud? Me?* he thought in a panic.

Nancy cleared her throat. "Well, since I'm the oldest here today, I'll go first. I'm thankful that the Lord sent me so many good friends to help get me through this year's tough times, and for my wonderful grandchildren who keep my own child alive just by being."

Trent saw Maggie's lower lip quiver, but before things turned maudlin Daniel spoke into the silence and shifted everyone's emotions to the opposite end of the spectrum. He piously bowed his head and folded his hands. "I'd like to thank You for Mrs. White, and 'specially for her great fluffer-nutter sandwiches!"

Trent heard Maggie's unladylike snort as Mickey spoke up. "I'd like to thank You for helping me walk again."

Rachel closed her eyes, pressed her palms and fingertips together and tilted her face to the heavens. "Thank You, Jesus, for Uncle Trent and Aunt Maggie guarding us, 'cause Mickey says they didn't have to guard us at all if they didn't want to. And I know You had to be the one to make them want to 'cause we're an awful lot of trouble."

Grace piped up next. "Tank You for my bear to hug."

Trent looked around and found himself speaking. "Thank You for my new family, and for bringing Maggie and me back together," he said, and was surprised that he actually meant it as a prayer.

He'd begun to understand a little more about God and what Jim and Maggie called a personal relationship with Jesus. It no longer meant weakness to him. He just wasn't sure what it did mean or how it applied to him. And so he spent time with Jim Dillon—no weakling, to be sure—questioning him casually on the Bible and church doctrine while they hammered, sawed and painted. He went to church with the family every Sunday, listening and evaluating everything he heard and saw.

"Grace Margaret Osborne! Put down that fork,"

Mickey hollered, startling Trent out of his ponderous thoughts. "Mom-Mom and Aunt Maggie haven't prayed yet."

Mickey sounded just like Maggie when someone was in big trouble. Trent looked at her and had to choke back laughter when he saw her fighting a smile. Mickey was a sensitive, funny kid with an overblown sense of responsibility toward his siblings. He'd come home the day before Halloween insisting that he walk into the house on his own. The whole family had gathered to celebrate his slow but triumphant entry. While his gait was still a little slow, with his whirl-wind personality he'd caused several changes in the household equilibrium and had completed their family.

Other things had changed as well. Trent had indeed decided to sell CSD, so he had a lot of spare time these days. And he'd used that time to make incredible strides on the house. There was still a little cosmetic work to be done inside, and some gingerbread trim for the porches and eaves still had to be restored, but the grand old lady was safe for the children, and nearly done. Her exterior was now painted a creamy taupe, the window sashes and gingerbread a deep barn red that contrasted nicely with rich forest-green trim.

Even though Maggie wanted someday to put up Victorian reproduction wallpaper, in order to give the place a more finished look for the holidays, Trent had painted the interior walls. One day when Maggie was out with Claire and the children, he and Jim had raided the still-to-be-finished third floor and liberated all the furniture Michael had stored up there for safety during the first-floor renovations. The derelict was now not only the grand old lady of Mike's vision, but she was a home as well. Truly Paradise Found.

Thoughts of Mike brought another stab of guilt. Trent knew he didn't deserve this kind of happiness. And it seemed that his life had been incredibly blessed because of his brother's death.

"Tomorrow, suppose we load up the van with a picnic lunch and drive up to the Poconos? Would everybody like to help cut a Christmas tree?" Trent asked, remembering Mike's tradition with his family. He wanted his brother's kids—at least the older three—to remember Mike. Continuing a family tradition seemed like a good way to keep his memory alive.

The next morning, Trent found that his Thanksgiving peace was still wrapping him in contentment. He grinned at Maggie as the doorbell chimed, and she handed him the spoon to continue dishing hot cereal.

The next moment he heard her cry, "Oh, sweet Lord! No!"

"Mickey, could you hand the bowls around?" he asked the boy.

"Sure," Mickey said, and jumped up to take Trent's place at the counter.

Maggie was standing on the porch outside the open front door staring as a car moved away down the drive. In her hand was an ominous blue-backed bundle of paper. "Mag?"

She turned, her face pale. There was terror in her eyes. "I thought he was a salesman. I felt sorry for him because he seemed so nervous. Then he handed it to me and took off. They did it.'' she said, her voice shaking. ''They really did it.'' The despair in her voice slashed at his heart.

Trent walked across the porch. ''Who did what?'' he asked, but he was afraid he already knew.

She handed him the crumpled notice. ''Your parents. They're suing for custody.''

Trent stared down at the document. Anger tore through him, shredding the blanket of happiness that had settled over his life these past days. Would they never be what he needed? Do what he needed? How could two people live their whole lives and never learn to think about what their actions did to others?

Then fear and guilt rushed in and nearly stole his breath. He and Maggie could lose the children! If they did, his parents would destroy everything wonderful about them. He knew that with a certainty. And if they lost the children to his parents, Maggie would have every reason to blame him. These were his parents, after all. Whether they were his naturally or by decree, he'd still brought them into her life. He was afraid he could easily lose her as well as the kids.

Trent looked over at Maggie and forgot himself. She was devastated. ''They don't have a chance,'' he told her, hoping he sounded more confident than he felt. He moved closer to her and enveloped her in his arms.

Maggie nodded and wrapped her arms around his waist. ''No chance. No. You're right,'' she said, and seemed to grow a little taller. Stand a little straighter. ''I'm sure they don't. But pray with me. Please.''

Trent not only wouldn't have denied her anything at that moment, but he was no longer sure that the God of the universe was just a casual observer. And he'd take any help he could get right about then. For all their sakes.

Maggie nestled her head under his chin and began her prayer. "Lord. You know our pain right now. You know our fear. And we know You're in control in this situation just as You are in all the moments and aspects of our lives. All we ask is the strength to bear this trial with grace and wisdom. We ask Your peace. Guide all of us in the best way to handle this both in court and with the children. We ask Your everlasting compassion to help us find it within our hearts to forgive these misguided people who have brought this pain and fear to us. Thank You, Lord. We do humbly praise You. Amen."

Maggie looked up at him, a small smile tugging at her lips. "They aren't going to win. We've come so far with God's help. We just have to travel a little farther. But we have a big decision to make. Do we tell the kids?"

"I say we tell them." Trent didn't know where the answer came from, but it was the right one.

Maggie looked as surprised as he felt. "But why worry them unnecessarily? Your parents can't win, Trent. Michael and Sarah even put a clause in their wills about our guardianship!"

"I think we need to tell them because if I've learned one thing dealing with these kids, it's that they're smart. How will they feel if they somehow hear about this? We can't take a chance that they won't find out. We surely can't risk letting them think we'd lie to them.''

Maggie nodded slowly. ''You're right. This isn't like letting them believe in Santa. It's about real trust. Now the question is, how do we tell them?''

''Right now, I think I'll call Ed and tell him the other shoe really dropped. Then we go chop down a tree. We'll tell the older kids when we get home.''

''That's perfect. Look,'' Maggie said, leaning closer and pointing to the court date. ''The hearing's scheduled for December twenty-third.''

''How could they do this to kids at Christmas?''

''I don't know, but that isn't what I'm talking about. Don't you see? Getting a tree will show the kids how confident we are that they'll still be with us come Christmas!'' A loud squeal from Grace in the kitchen drew their attention. Maggie chuckled. ''I'd better get back in there before we have an uprising on our hands.''

Maggie rushed back inside, but Trent didn't move. He knew it was chilly for shirtsleeves but he didn't feel the cold. He was numb with fear. What if they lost?

Chapter Thirteen

Maggie closed the laundry room door as Trent came out of Grace's room. He smiled, but it was a nervous smile. "She's waiting for you to kiss her good-night. Don't let her con you. She's had a drink of water and two stories."

"The others are in their rooms. Trent, maybe we should wait. Just 'til tomorrow. After they've had a good night's sleep." Maggie didn't want to have to do this. She didn't want any of this to be happening. Not because she didn't have confidence in the Lord's protection, but because she could see through Trent's supposed confidence. He was scared to death and feeling guilty because it was his parents causing the trouble. And if the children reacted badly, he'd feel even worse.

Trent pursed his lips, then after a moment's thought shook his head. "Mag, it has to be now. Ed should be here in less than an hour. Suppose they hear us talking? They've all had a full day. They'll sleep even after we tell them. Try not to worry." He put his arms around her and gave her a quick squeeze. Maggie leaned into him, wanting to give him the strength he thought he needed to give to her. He looked down, and as often happened when they touched, time seemed to suspend its hold on them. Trent brought one hand up and traced her features in a feather-light caress ending with her lips. Then, on a quick intake of breath he covered her tingling lips with his own. It was a kiss that turned desperate before he suddenly released her.

Maggie stared up at him, her heart racing, knowing with a certainty what caused the haunted look she saw reflected in his blue eyes. "It's not your fault, Trent. None of it. You didn't pick your parents any more than Michael did. This is their doing. I don't blame you for it."

He nodded but looked unconvinced. "Go tuck Grace in, and meet us in the family room. Okay?"

It was Maggie's turn to nod. She'd have to convince him some other way. Why could he not trust in her love?

The two-year-old had already fallen asleep by the time Maggie went into her room, so she straightened the covers and said a quick prayer for the little cherub. As she entered the hall, Trent came out of Mickey's room with the other three children.

Mickey looked up, his big brown eyes worried and apprehensive. "Is everything okay, Aunt Maggie?"

Trent was right about telling them, because at least Mickey had already figured out that something was wrong. But she purposely misunderstood the boy anyway, hoping to give him a few more minutes' peace. "Are you kidding? She's already in dreamland."

"I didn't mean Grace. I meant—"

"Let's go downstairs before we wake her up," Trent cut in. He scooped up Daniel, who was dead on his little four-year-old feet, and hurried the procession along down the hall and the back stairs.

"So what's up?" Mickey, spokesman for the little group, asked as all three climbed up onto the family room sofa.

Trent sat down opposite the kids in a big overstuffed chair that faced the sofa, and Maggie perched on the arm next to him. "It's nothing we want you kids to worry about," she said, draping her arm over Trent's shoulders, "but we felt you should know what's going on."

Trent took over, thankfully saying the words Maggie wasn't sure she could say. "My parents—your dad's mother and father—want you to come live with them. They aren't happy that Aunt Maggie and I were named your guardians."

"But we want you to guard us," Rachel said. "I don't want to go live with her. She said I was rude, and she doesn't like Cindy." The ever-present baby doll got a tight protective squeeze.

Maggie saw tears in Rachel's golden-brown eyes. "We didn't say you're going to live with them, sweetie. Just that it's what *they* want," she quickly assured Rachel.

"We already told them in no uncertain terms in Florida right after the accident that we wouldn't let them have you. So they've gone to the court and have begun what's called suing for custody."

"Uncle Ed's a lawyer. You should call him," Mickey advised sagely.

Trent smiled. "Already done, pal, but thanks for the advice. He's been working for months just in case they did this. He knows just what to do, so don't you kids worry."

Mickey narrowed his dark eyes. Clearly angry, he said, "I bet they waited 'til I could walk and I wasn't a burden anymore. I won't go live with them. Not after what they said about me and Daddy. I'll run away."

"Me, too!" Rachel added in her most defiant tone.

"None of that's going to be necessary. We aren't going to let it happen," Trent told the three. He leaned forward, elbows braced on his knees.

Maggie let her hand trail down his back and slid forward, unwilling to break their contact. "And more important," she added, "the Lord isn't going to let it happen."

"So, what happens next? Do we have to go into court? Will there be a jury and a judge?" Mickey asked.

"It'll just be a judge. Uncle Ed will present evidence that your mom and dad wanted us to take care of you. Then Aunt Maggie and I will testify—that means we'll tell our side," Trent explained.

Mickey jumped up. "I want to, too!" Mickey demanded. "I want to tell my side!" Maggie had never seen the boy so angry. She looked at Trent to see his reaction. She'd wanted to protect the children from all of this, but Trent probably had a better perspective on how Mickey would feel.

"Why do you want to testify?" Trent asked.

"Because I want to live here with you and Aunt Maggie. If it's about where we live, we should get to say how we feel. I don't like them. They made me feel bad. You and Aunt Maggie wouldn't ever have talked about me like they did."

Trent folded his hands and steepled his index fingers against his lips. He just stared ahead, silent. Finally he nodded. "Aunt Maggie and I will talk it over with Uncle Ed when he comes over later tonight. It's very brave of you to want to do this."

"I—I could, too," Rachel said, but sounded unsure. Then fire came into her eyes. "She said somebody should burn Cindy! I don't like them and I don't want to live with them. I like it here!"

"And this is where you'll stay," Maggie said with deepest conviction. "Don't you worry about it. It's very brave of you both to offer, but Uncle Ed might say it isn't necessary. We'll all think about it."

"Can I go to bed now?" Daniel said. He sounded a tinge angry, too, and Maggie realized that he hadn't said a word until then. Trent, too, must have realized. "That's the first thing you've had to say about all of this, partner. What do you think about it?"

Daniel folded his arms, looking even more mutinous. "I think that I don't know why everybody sounds so surprised." He stood and put his hands on his hips. "Why did any of you guys think nothing bad was going to happen? I knew it, and you both made me think I was wrong, but now I know I was right. Nothing good *doesn't* get wrecked around here. You're all stupid!'' Before Maggie or Trent could react to his outburst, Daniel took off and ran up the steps.

Trent jumped up. "I'll go. It was my idea to tell him," he said, guilt weighing down his very words.

I knew this was a mistake! Sharper than she meant to sound, Maggie said, "No, I'll go! You wait for Ed." Standing and putting a restraining hand on Trent's arm, she added, "Come on, kids. Let's hit the wooden hill. It's been a long day."

Mickey and Rachel both looked for a long moment at her, then stopped in front of Trent, who stood looking both thunderstruck and crushed. Rachel reached up and patted Trent's big callused hand as if he were the most delicate of creatures. "We're glad you told us, Uncle Trent. And one of us would have forgot and told Daniel, so it was a good thing you told him, too. He'll be okay." She sighed and shook her head, adding, "He just gets weird sometimes."

"I'll let him sleep with me," Mickey said, looking at Maggie. "That always works. Night-night." Both children turned away as if it were a rehearsed movement and climbed the stairs, hand in hand.

"Should I go?" she asked Trent, now suddenly unsure what was right and what was wrong.

Trent sat down and once again leaned his elbows on his knees, only this time he buried his face in his hands. "How the heck should I know? You as much as said it. I heard it in your voice. You think I was wrong about telling them."

"I thought for a minute you were, but..." She

sighed and shook her head. "Now I'm not sure. Mickey and Rachel certainly don't think telling them was wrong. We'll just have to get Daniel through the next month as best we can. Try to remember that his upset is your parents' fault, not yours. Time and the Lord will teach him that bad things sometimes happen to good people, but not always. I—"

The doorbell rang, halting her words. Trent stood to go to the door, but Maggie grabbed his arm. "No, wait. I need to say this. I'm sorry I doubted you. I'm sorry I snapped at you."

Trent stared at her for a moment, then nodded. "It's okay. I doubted me, too."

"I guess all parents do. It must come with the territory."

The doorbell rang again. "I'd better get that before he has all of them all back down here," Trent said.

Maggie waited for the two men in the kitchen. She put on water for tea and got a pen and paper out of the drawer of the recipe center in case she needed to take notes. She heard their muted voices in the dining room. The kettle was whistling when the quiet talk stopped and the swinging door pushed open.

"Hi, Maggie," Ed said, peeking around the door.

"Thanks for coming over." She held a mug aloft. "Earl Grey?"

"Great! Trent went up to check on the kids. He said you told the older three. It was a good move. I've found it's not good to keep kids in the dark. They almost always find out what's going on somehow. The caseworker usually tips it off."

"Caseworker?"

"I think I mentioned this. The court will order a home study done on both your home and the Osbornes'."

They both sat down at the big oak kitchen table. "Thank the Lord, Trent worked as hard as he did on the house," Maggie said, looking around at what had once been the only finished area of the downstairs. "A war zone wouldn't have made a very good impression. But now the house is a plus compared to Trent's parents' house. I mean, who would put children in that mausoleum where they live?"

Ed took a sip of tea and shook his shaggy head. "They're smarter than that. They've already called in a decorator. Can't you just hear Albertine," In a nasal drawl he added, "'Give it a homey look, my dear, but not too country. I can't abide country.'"

Maggie grinned at his impersonation of Trent's mother, but she didn't feel much like laughing. She hadn't thought Trent's parents would go to such lengths.

"How did you find that out so quickly?" Trent asked from the doorway. "I only called you this morning." He walked as far as the table and leaned his forearms on the back of her chair.

Ed comically raised and lowered his eyebrows. "How long have I known your parents? I've been sort of keeping tabs on them, because basically I don't trust them," Ed admitted, his smile mischievous. "My mother's keeping an eye out. I asked her to tell me if she noticed anything unusual. She called me today to tell me they were having one of those wooden swing sets erected in their yard. And that a decorator's truck was parked in the drive.''

"Unbelievable," Trent said, shaking his head.

"Well, you'd better believe it. This isn't going to be a cakewalk. They'll pull out all the stops. Look at the court date they set. They don't care whom they hurt as long as they have their way.''

"Even if it's four innocent children who get hurt," Trent said, and stalked to the window over the sink. He looked out over the yard. He could put in one of those big wooden things, but he didn't want the kids caught in some sort of game of one-upmanship between him and his parents. The children would be the ones in the middle and they'd be smart enough to realize it. "So what do we do, other than play keep-up with the elder Osbornes?" he asked as he walked back to the table.

Ed looked up. "You present your family to the caseworker just the way it is. You let her meet Claire White and outline her duties, and again you let the caseworker see the relationship Claire has built with the kids. And I'll file for a continuance. I doubt the judge will object to postponing the hearing until after Christmas.''

"Aren't you going to be ready by the twenty-third?" Maggie asked, frowning.

"Oh, I'm nearly ready today.''

"Then, I don't think you should ask for a postponement," she said.

Now it was Ed's turn to frown. "Maggie, not that I think it'll happen, you understand, but if by some rotten twist of fate they win, the kids would be up-rooted and with strangers for Christmas.''

''But as you said, it isn't going to happen. It needs to be over with. We've told them and we can't have it hanging over their heads or ours.''

''Are you sure, Mag?'' Trent asked. He wondered, then knew immediately, where her strength came from. He wished he had just a smidgen of the confidence her faith gave her.

Maggie reached out her hand and pulled him into the chair next to her. ''It's going to be all right.''

''Okay, then, you two. We'll let the hearing date stand. Let's get started. I want you both to know what to expect. But I have to know what to expect from their lawyer. Is there anything that could come out in court that would make either or both of you look unfit in the eyes of the court?''

Maggie looked sad and horribly guilty. ''They can use my leaving Trent, can't they?''

But it was my fault, too. Trent sucked in a quick breath, thinking he'd spoken aloud. But when no one looked at him, he realized that it had been his guilty conscience speaking silently. He should tell her. But now, when his parents were threatening to take the kids, would be the worst timing. And he didn't have to risk it at all. It didn't matter anymore. It couldn't.

''Trent?'' Ed called out a little loudly.

Trent snapped out of his musings and realized that they were both staring at him. ''What? Sorry, my mind wandered.''

''Is there anything I need to know?''

Trent shrugged. ''Nothing I can think of, and as far

as the divorce, my parents don't know what split us up."

"Well, that's good. I'd hate to have to explain that you two almost broke up over adoption."

Again Trent's guilt swelled up and threatened to choke him. How much harder would it be to refute his not having wanted any children at all? He'd never thought he'd be glad for the rift that had divided his family for years, but he was supremely grateful for it at that moment. His parents knew nothing of his personal life.

Ed went over what the court procedure would be like, then got into what he intended to present to the court. "I want you to know that besides the will, I have the letter Albertine sent to Sarah. I'm going to introduce it into evidence to prove how unsuitable they are as parents. And you're going to have to testify about your childhood with them, Trent. I also have to tell you that I think I may need to call at least Mickey, and maybe even Rachel, if I think the judge is leaning the wrong way. I'll avoid it if I can. If not, I'll suggest the judge talk to the kids in chambers."

"I hate this." Maggie slapped her palm on the arm of her chair. "I hate involving them!"

Trent felt his heart twist at her distress. "I'm so sorry, Mag."

Maggie reached across the table and grasped his hand. "It isn't your fault!"

Ed stood. "Look, we've covered enough for tonight. You two look beat. Try to relax. It's going to be fine."

"I know it is," Maggie told Ed, then stood. "Are

you sure you have to run off? I've got cake to go with the tea.''

Ed picked up his mug and gulped down the rest of his tea. ''Nah. You guys get some sleep. We'll get together again soon.''

Trent walked with Ed to the front door. ''You really think we can win?''

Ed stepped off the porch onto the first step, then pivoted and looked up. ''I don't see a reason you should lose, but that's no guarantee. Your father still throws money at problems, and he hired Jason Wright. He's considered a big gun. On the other hand, I see your mother as their big weak point—like sending that letter to Sarah. If I can bring out that aspect of her personality, we shouldn't have a problem.''

''She isn't that stupid. She'll know what to say.''

''You leave that up to me. Now go spend some time with your pretty wife and try to forget about this.''

He waited on the porch until Ed turned out of the lane. Then, hands jammed in his pockets, Trent went back inside and looked around the entranceway. The woodwork gleamed as did the chandelier hanging from the high ceiling. His gaze trailed back down the stairs, noting with pride the way the banister's smooth curves shone in the light. He smiled a little as his gaze came to rest on a battered red toy truck that lay next to the stairs where Daniel had abandoned it sometime during the day. He picked it up and made his way to the kitchen. He glanced into the family room. There, too, was evidence of children. Of happiness. Then a little piece of faded pink satin and lace peeked out from the front edge of the sofa, drawing his eye.

Trent walked in and dug Rachel's doll out from between the cushions. He stared at it, bewildered. Rachel never went to bed without Cindy. She rarely went anywhere but to school without her beloved baby doll. Why, on a night when she needed her security more than ever, would she leave it behind? Trent frowned. No, she hadn't just left it. She'd stuffed it out of sight. Hidden it!

"Why, Rachel?" he whispered to the empty room.

Chapter Fourteen

Trent quickly handled locking up, and took the stairs two at a time. He tiptoed into Rachel's room, softly lit by the night-light Maggie had added after the accident to reassure a six-year-old who was suddenly afraid of the dark.

The light caught her tousled reddish-blond hair, bringing out its red highlights. Trent felt a smile tug at his lips when he saw her scrunched-tight eyes as she feigned sleep. When he'd checked in on her earlier he had only looked in from the doorway, or he would have realized that she'd never gone to sleep.

"I know you're awake, angel," he whispered as he sat down on the bed next to her.

Her eyes popped open. "Hi, Daddy," she said.

Trent felt a pain so sharp that he nearly gasped, wishing with everything in him that he could change places with Mike. Were his brother alive, these children wouldn't be in any danger. He'd never felt as worthless in his life as he did at that moment. "No, angel, it's only Uncle Trent. You forgot Cindy. How come you left her behind?"

Even in the low lighting he could see the sadness written in Rachel's eyes. "I thought I ought to get used to not having her. Just in case. I know *she* wouldn't let me keep her."

"Your grandmother just doesn't understand how much you love Cindy," Trent told her as he nestled the doll in the crook of Rachel's arm. Before he could pull his hand away, he felt the doll get a welcoming squeeze. "But you don't have to worry about having to leave Cindy behind," he continued as he pushed a strawberry-blond lock off her forehead. "Uncle Ed is a great lawyer. And God is on our side, just as Aunt Maggie says. You aren't going anywhere. Now you and Cindy better get some sleep. We have to dig the Christmas decorations out of the attic tomorrow and see what we have to work with. Then we have to go out and buy some more for the outside. This year, Paradise Found gets decorated the way she deserves."

Rachel nodded and nestled down into her pillows and covers with Cindy, closing her eyes. Trent leaned down and kissed her on the forehead. "Night-night, angel," he whispered, and stood.

A smile bloomed on Rachel's bow lips and she opened her big dark eyes again. The sadness and fear he'd seen before were gone. "Night-night, Daddy," she whispered back, and closed her eyes slowly.

Trent stood in complete shock. It hadn't been a

mistake. She'd called him Daddy, not once but twice. Through a sheen of tears, he somehow managed to get out into the hall. His composure somewhat restored, he checked on the others, all sleeping soundly, then made his way to his and Maggie's room.

When he entered, the room was bathed in soft light from a pair of wall sconces. He found Maggie sitting in bed wearing a lacy nightgown. "Is something else wrong, or is it more of the same?" she asked.

Trent shrugged and walked over to sit on the bed. She looked so beautiful that she nearly took his breath, but then he remembered her questions and a torrent of emotion threatened to overwhelm him once again.

"Rachel," he said, but the word sounded rusty and caught in his throat. He cleared his throat, trying to fight tears of overwhelming joy and supreme confusion that threatened to erupt. He hated that Maggie had seen him cry that morning in Florida, and now he feared it would happen again. He didn't want Maggie to lose all respect for him, and what quicker way was there for a man to broadcast his weakness than tears?

"Rachel," he tried again, and forced himself to continue this time when his voice broke a little. "Rachel left Cindy downstairs. When I went into her room to put it in bed with her, she called me 'Daddy.'" He stopped and cleared his throat. "I thought she'd mixed me up with Mike at first, but she hadn't. She meant it. I feel... Maggie I don't know what I feel. All these emotions are bombarding me.'' He hastily swiped at a tear that got past his guard.

''Don't,'' she said and grabbed his hand, doing the job herself so gently that she nearly destroyed him right there and then. ''Tears aren't a sin.''

Trent found he had to look away from her kind eyes. ''The way I was raised they were.''

Maggie stared at Trent's bowed head and realized for the first time just how much damage Royce and Albertine were responsible for in their elder son. Their effect on Michael had always been obvious, but Trent seemed to have left his childhood and his parents in the past. She'd never seen a hint that they'd had any effect on him at all, except his penchant for processing hurt into anger.

She recalled that morning in the hospital in Florida when Albertine had criticized him for creating a scene. He hadn't shown hurt, but had typically put her in her place with a few choice words. But now, after all these years, Maggie understood. The anger didn't heal the hurt, it just covered it up.

She felt remorse that she hadn't understood before. In her own defense, though, she and Trent had had very little to do with the elder Osbornes over the years. His parents' shabby treatment of Sarah had effectively removed them from Trent and Maggie's world as well Michael's, so Maggie hadn't seen the immediate effects their continued presence might have revealed. But he had been scarred by every little cut over the years. He'd just never openly revealed those scars. Until now.

Maggie reached out and ran her fingers through his hair. "Do you know the shortest verse in the Bible?"

He looked up at her, his eyebrows drawn together in a *V*. "No."

She smiled gently at his obvious confusion. "'Jesus wept.' That's the verse. Those two words show so much about Him and teach one of His greatest lessons. It shows how much of a human being He was and how deeply He loves us. The lesson is that it doesn't make a man less of a man because he shows his feelings.

"Jesus of Nazareth was no wimp. He was a carpenter back in the days when that meant chopping down a tree by yourself and dragging it back to your shop. Then cutting and splitting it with hand tools before you could make it into something. It was his Godhood that people back then doubted, not his manhood."

"I never thought of it like that, but I guess you're right."

Maggie leaned forward and kissed him. "I don't think you're weak because being called Daddy by a child you love brought tears to your eyes. I think you're wonderful. I love who you are. And I also don't blame you because your parents are like a couple of spoiled children who try to take whatever they want regardless of who gets hurt in the process."

"Are you sure?"

Maggie sighed at the doubt in his voice, and kissed him again. This time she put her heart into the meet-

ing of their lips. She would just have to show him
how much she loved the man he was.

"Everybody, come get lunch," Trent heard Maggie
call out just as he hung the last light on the tree. The
plan was for the family to gather after they ate in the
big front parlor, and hang the decorations on the big
Douglas fir they'd cut the day after Thanksgiving.

He'd spent some time that morning rehearsing with
Grace how to put the angel atop the tree. So far she'd
mastered putting a plastic ring over the top branch, a
birthday hat and a paper cup. But putting an angel on
top of a Christmas tree was a lot trickier, and Trent
wasn't sure he and his littlest assistant had mastered
it. He hoped she was up to the challenge. As the
youngest in the family, tradition said Grace should
put the angel on top of the tree as soon as she was
able. Daniel, unhappy with being displaced from this
last special role as baby of the family, was Grace's
disgruntled backup.

Trent stepped out from behind the tree, nearly fell
over Mickey and got tangled in the light cord, pulling
it out of the wall socket. The lights went out, the tree
wobbled a bit, and Trent made a frantic grab to steady
it. "Sorry, kiddo. Didn't see you there," he told the
boy. He took a deep breath and let it out slowly to
calm his pounding heart.

Mickey hung his head. "Sorry, I guess I got underfoot."

Since the night they'd told them about the custody
suit, all three children had reacted differently. Mickey

was rarely more than one step behind Trent. He'd decided to become Trent's little helper. Unfortunately, he was often getting underfoot and had caused more than one near disaster or minor injury to Trent because of it.

By day, Rachel acted as if all was well, but the nightmares about the accident that had plagued her at summer's end had returned with a vengeance. Neither Trent nor Maggie had managed an unbroken night's sleep since.

And Daniel had become a little monster—and that description was kind. He teased and tormented Grace, taking toys from the toddler that he couldn't possibly want to play with. He had even hidden Cindy from Rachel for two days; when asked why, he'd rolled his eyes and spat back that it was stinky and dirty.

Maggie thought his behavior was his way of acting out his anger at his grandparents. Trent figured it could be that but maybe something more, too, since most of his anger seemed to be directed at Maggie. At this point, if Daniel verbally attacked her again, Trent was going to step in and have a serious talk— husband to four-year-old tormentor.

Trent ruffled Mickey's hair. "It's okay. No harm done. But listen, my back's killing me from standing on the ladder. Suppose you climb back under and plug them in for me."

Maggie slid the parlor doors open just as Mickey disappeared under the thick bottom branches of the Christmas tree. She stuck her head in. "You two coming? Soup's on. Oh, the lights are gorgeous!'' she exclaimed, and came into the room.

Trent grinned. It was his first eleven-foot Christmas tree. Actually, he and Maggie had always opted for a fake four-footer, so this was his first real Christmas tree, period. He was as excited as the kids. ''Thank you, Mrs. Osborne. And it's ready for ornaments right on schedule, thanks to the help of my able assistant. Come on out here, able assistant.''

''It looks wonderful, Mickey,'' she said. ''I've got all sorts of Christmas music lined up in the CD changer, and hot cider and cookies ready for our tree-trimming party after lunch. The turkey soup's already dished. Let's go, you two. We've got a tree to trim.''

As they entered the kitchen following Mickey, Trent watched in shock as Daniel pressed his index finger down on the side of his bowl and purposely tipped it over.

''Oh, my,'' Maggie cried, and rushed to mop up the mess. ''I don't have any more soup left. Oh, well. Don't worry about it, dear. Accidents happen. You can have mine, and I'll just heat up some of that tomato soup I like so much.''

''No, you will not eat canned soup after you spent all that time making homemade. He did that on purpose,'' Trent said, gritting his teeth. ''Didn't you, Daniel?''

''Yeah,'' Daniel spat back, a defiant expression on his face.

Maggie looked shocked and wounded. ''Why?'' she asked.

Daniel ignored her and directed his answer to Trent. "I hate her soup. She doesn't make it like my mom did. I'd rather eat peanut butter and jelly. At least she can't wreck that."

"That's it! Go to your room, boy," Trent ordered.

"Trent—"

"No, Mag. He's gone after you for the last time." He looked at Daniel, who sat with his mouth gaping open in shock. "Did you hear me? Go up to your room. Now! I'll be up after I've eaten, and we'll talk about this and the rest of your behavior lately. I, for one, have had it!"

Daniel's lip quivered. "But I'm hungry."

"You should have thought of that before dumping a bowl of perfectly good soup all over for your aunt to clean up."

"I'm sorry! I won't do it again," Daniel rushed to promise.

"Too late. March," Trent ordered.

Lunch, far from the celebration Maggie had planned, was a subdued affair. Trent was sorry he'd had to spoil the meal, but enough was enough, and dealing with Daniel had been too important to put off any longer. After they'd eaten, Maggie had decided to put on a Christmas video to watch with the other children while Trent went up to talk to Daniel.

He found the boy sitting in the corner of his room, clutching a tattered blanket that Trent hadn't seen in years.

"Are you going to spank me?"

Trent was so surprised by the question that he sank to the bed and simply stared at the forlorn little boy. Spanking was one of those subjects he and Maggie had discussed at length. They both had the same opinion. If any alternative punishment would alter a child's destructive or dangerous behavior, one shouldn't resort to spanking.

Trent couldn't think of a punishment he hadn't tried, but spanking still seemed like the wrong approach. He knew it was the custody suit causing Daniel's bad conduct, so therefore it was Royce and Albertine's fault—not Daniel's.

"I guess you're pretty scared," Trent commented.

"I never been spanked. My friend in nursery school says it hurts. A lot!"

Trent sighed, hoping to bring the discussion back to Daniel's behavior. "Well, you won't find out now because I'm not going to spank you for spilling your soup." He paused, watching Daniel intently. "I meant, I bet you're scared about the custody suit. But, Daniel, I will not have you attacking Aunt Maggie. She loves you. She takes care of you. And all you've done for two weeks is make her life and the lives of your brother and sisters miserable. Why?"

"It will hurt," Daniel said in a pain-filled whisper.

"I already promised not to spank you," Trent repeated.

Daniel shook his head. "It'll hurt when I have to go live with them. 'Cause I love you and Aunt Maggie, and it'll hurt like when Mommy and Daddy died if I can't live with you anymore."

Confused, Trent urged, "And so you're being mean to Maggie and your brother and sisters because…?"

"'Cause then you and Aunt Maggie will always be mad at me and punish me, and I won't miss you so much when I have to leave. But I didn't want to make you so mad that you'd spank me. I really, really didn't mean to make you that mad." His little freckled face crumpled then and a sob burst forth. Trent was on his knees in a heartbeat with Daniel clasped to his chest.

Maggie woke sometime in the night, and a feeling of aloneness engulfed her. She rolled over and reached out for Trent but he was gone, his pillow cool. When he didn't return after several minutes, Maggie tossed off her covers and pulled on her robe to go in search of him.

She found him in the front parlor, sitting on the overstuffed sofa, staring up at the lit tree. Its ornaments sparkled against the deep green curtain of fragrant pine.

"It turned out beautifully, didn't it?" she said. Bright. Noisy. Joyful. And a little hectic in places. Maggie saw the tree as a concrete symbol of their new family. Created by the combination of Michael and Sarah's ornaments and the ones Maggie and Trent had collected over the years, the tree was a harmony of color and lights, just as the family they'd fashioned was a perfect symphony of love and happiness.

Trent nodded, his head tipped to the side a bit as he stared up at the tree. "The angel's still a little lopsided, but Grace did a bang-up job getting it up there, didn't she?''

Maggie thought of the picture she'd taken of Trent standing on the ladder holding Grace up to put the angel on top of the tree, both of them wearing their brightest smiles. Grace's happy squeals of accomplishment, and Trent's laughter still echoed in her mind. She chuckled. ''Except that now she thinks the Christmas angel's called a 'put on.'''

''We'll work on that next,'' Trent said.

The hollow sound of his voice tweaked Maggie's radar. She studied him in the low light of the tree's many tiny lights. ''Trent? What is it?''

''What if they aren't here for Christmas, Mag? What if my parents get them?''

''They'll be with us. Please have faith.''

Trent pursed his lips and shook his head. ''I wish I could. Believe me, I wish I could. But God let my parents have Mike and me. So my mind tells me it can happen again to these kids. And my heart's so busy being scared that I can't seem to catch my breath half the time. Everything was going so well.''

''And it will again,'' Maggie promised as she snuggled next to him. Hugging his arm, she dropped her head on his shoulder. ''We'll be sitting here on Christmas night, exhausted, toys scattered all around, the kids asleep and us too tired to go up the stairs.''

''How can you be so sure?'' he whispered, his voice breaking on the last word.

''I don't know. Somehow, my faith assures me that

it will all turn out fine, even though we might have to walk through the fire first.''

Trent sighed. ''I just don't have that kind of trust to give, Maggie. I wish I did. Someday maybe I will, but not right now.''

The flash of understanding left Maggie stunned. It was a lack of trust that held him back from committing to the Lord. He couldn't trust Him any more than he was able to trust her. And it was all her fault. She had broken Trent's trust when she broke their marriage vows by leaving him, and now she felt as if her own heart would break. She was very much afraid that it was the memory of her faithlessness that kept him from embracing the Lord and His life-giving faith.

Maggie sat up and scooted around to face Trent. Tears flooded her eyes. ''Oh, Trent, I took so much from you when I left. I'm sorry. I'll prove you can trust again, somehow.''

Trent's eyes widened with something akin to panic. ''No, Maggie, it isn't your fault! Please don't blame yourself. Please. I've forgiven that. It's forgotten. My problem is that every time I've become secure in my life something happens to show me that it's all smoke and mirrors. Most of those times were my own parents' doing. Nannies who made me feel loved fired with no warning. Family vacations canceled out of the blue. Shipping me off to Ruxley. Graduations they didn't show up for. Just like now. They come out of the woodwork with this suit just when I thought they'd given up the idea.''

"Trent, I know your parents betrayed your trust, but Jesus isn't going to betray you! I failed you, too, but He won't. He isn't a flawed being the way we are."

"But that's just it, Mag. I feel as if every time something has gone wrong He *has* betrayed me, because He let it happen."

"No. It's the people in your life. He's given us free will, and with it we've made choices that hurt you. Myself included. You may have forgiven me but that doesn't change what I did. I'm going to keep praying that Jesus will reveal Himself to you so you can place your trust in Someone who'll never fail you the way I did."

Chapter Fifteen

Trent squeezed Maggie's hand as they entered the courtroom. He heard her take a deep breath before she started down the center aisle. Still clasping her hand, he had no choice but to follow. All the children were with Nancy and Ester in an anteroom. The children were there because his parents had petitioned the court to have them immediately available to them after the hearing.

Ed had filed a counter-motion requesting that the children be excluded from the courtroom. The female judge had readily agreed, but her thoughtlessness in requiring their presence in the courthouse worried Trent to no end. Was she the kind of woman who didn't care if children were upset? Did that mean she wouldn't be bothered by the idea of forcing the children to live with virtual strangers? Or were they there so she could solicit their opinion?

Maggie and Sarah's mothers were with the children, not only to take care of them and to keep them calm, but also to testify if they were needed. Nancy Merritt's health worried both of them.

He and Maggie reached the front of the room, so Trent stepped aside to let her through the narrow break in the railing. Trent glanced at his parents and turned away, not sure he'd ever want to set eyes on either of them again after this.

Maggie moved to the farthest seat at the table where Ed was sitting alone, and Trent sat next to his friend and lawyer. Ed turned toward them, deliberately blocking the view of those at the plaintiffs' table. "I tried to reach you this morning but you'd left already," he said in a low voice.

Trent felt instant panic at Ed's tone. Ed never sounded worried without reason. "We had to swing by to pick up Ester and Nancy. Why were you trying to get hold of us?"

"Jason Wright added a name to their witness list—Nadine Morresey." Ed stared at him. "What does your old girlfriend have to do with custody of Mike's kids?"

The name rocked Trent to his core. "I don't get it. First, she wasn't really a girlfriend. More like a dinner companion. As far as I know my parents have never met her."

"They apparently have. I couldn't block her appearance, but I might be able to get a continuance," Ed suggested.

"No," Maggie said immediately. "We can't put this off. My mother just had to peel little Grace off me. Even she's feeling the tension. It's heartbreaking to see those precious little people frightened like this.''

Trent nodded. ''I agree, Ed. The kids can't stand this any longer. And I'm not sure about Maggie, but I can't either.''

''Okay,'' Ed said with a determined nod. ''The real point is, can Nadine hurt us? Think. What does she know that would help their case?'' Ed asked.

While a jumble of thoughts rushed through Trent's mind, Maggie replied, ''Trent dated her until the accident. Maybe they're trying to establish that he was going forward with the divorce until the children needed us.''

''If that's all she's here for, we'll just admit that you got back together for the kids' sake. There's really nothing wrong with that as long as you've worked through your differences. But—'' Ed dragged his hand through his hair and grimaced ''—Look, Trent, I hate to be so blunt, but how close were you and Nadine?''

Trent glanced at Maggie and put his arm around her. ''I don't see how they can make a moral issue out of this. I made her seem like more to Maggie when I was trying to push Maggie away, but she was never more than a friend. Anyway, Mag and I were legally separated, and I only saw Nadine socially. I was never unfaithful to my wife. I was never in Nadine's apartment. She invited me in, but the thought of it made me uncomfortable. She was only inside my place once. And that was before I ever took her out. She stopped by to see Maggie, and I told her Mag had left me a month earlier. After that, she called me once in a while to see how I was doing. A couple months later, I was so lonely that I asked her out for dinner.

"But that first night when she came by to see Maggie, I had fallen on the ice and was on painkillers and muscle relaxers. I woke up the next morning and couldn't remember the night before. It scared me to death, so I stopped the medicine. Later that day I did finally remember that she'd been there, but only because she called to see how I was. Man, I thought that scared me, but not knowing what I might have said to her scares me a lot more. Suppose I told her why Mag left me?"

"Well, there's nothing to do but think on our feet and try to counter anything she says as best we can," Ed said. He glanced past Maggie, nodding his head in that direction. "We're about to find out how well we do."

"All rise," the court bailiff called. "The court of Chester County, Commonwealth of Pennsylvania, is now in session. The Honorable Winifred T. Golden presiding." Trent stood, his stomach roiling. Maggie slid her hand into his and once again gave it a reassuring squeeze. He closed his eyes. *Please, God. Please.*

The bailiff announced the principles in the case, and Jason Wright stood to present his side of the argument. His opening statement held no surprises. Nor did his polished appearance or dramatic flare. He was well prepared and methodical.

Then it was Ed Hanson's turn. He approached the bench, his suit slightly rumpled, his hair as askew as ever. He had an aw-shucks demeanor that came across as unsophisticated and unfocused—and a mind like a steel trap. Nothing got past the man. He seemed to Trent to be the bar association's answer to Columbo.

Wright called his first witness: Nadine Morresey. Trent hadn't noticed her in the room because he'd been concentrating on the proceedings. She looked horrified to be there. As if she wanted to be anywhere else. She was well-dressed, and looking, as always, sweet and comforting. The very qualities that had drawn him to her in those dark days when he'd needed a friend.

The bailiff swore her in and asked her to state her name.

"Nadine Turner Morresey," she replied.

"Ms. Morresey, would you tell the court how you know Mr. and Mrs. Trenton Osborne?"

"I went to high school with Maggie—that's Mrs. Osborne. After she left Trent, he and I became very good friends."

"Oh, come now, Ms. Morresey. Friends?"

Nadine blushed. After a long hesitation she swallowed and said, *"Friends,"* with an embarrassed wobble in her voice.

Trent's blood reached the boiling point. He glanced at Maggie to gauge her reaction, but she seemed as serene as ever. Where did she find this ability to trust? Then he looked over at Ed, who had just scribbled the word *friends* on his yellow legal pad, then underlined it heavily several times.

"Were you aware that there was a reconciliation under discussion between them?" Wright asked.

Nadine blinked, clearly shocked by the question. "Yes. Uh. No, not really."

"Which is it, Ms. Morresey?" Wright asked.

"It hardly matters, Your Honor. Any answer would be hearsay," Ed called quietly.

"Sustained. Please stick only to facts Ms. Morresey can add," Judge Golden instructed Wright.

"Where did you think your relationship with Trenton Osborne *was headed*?"

"Headed?"

"Didn't you tell Albertine Osborne that you hoped to marry her son one day?"

Ed put a restraining hand on Trent's arm, or he would have shouted his own objection. He had never considered her as anything more than a friend.

Looking horribly embarrassed, she said, "I guess I said that but—"

"So this man, who was going to marry you, took you out for the last time when?"

"But—"

"When, Ms. Morresey?"

"The day before his brother died. Trent left on a business trip an hour after we had lunch."

"And at that time he was still going forward with the divorce?"

"Yes."

"When was it that you first learned of their reconciliation?" Wright asked.

"After Michael and Sarah's memorial service."

"Are you aware of the reason for the near end to their marriage?"

"Objection, Your Honor, we aren't here to dissect

the Osbornes' marriage,'' Ed called out before Nadine could open her mouth. ''I've let several hearsay remarks go by in the interest of time. Four youngsters are waiting to see if they'll have a Merry Christmas with the aunt and uncle they love,'' Ed added, making the point that the older Osbornes didn't seem to care. ''Ms. Morresey is hardly in a position to know the reason why these people separated. And we're willing to stipulate that one of the reasons for their reconciliation was the guardianship of the children. Perhaps that way he will stop badgering his own witness.''

What did I say that night? Trent thought, racking his brain and finding only what he had back then— fuzz! This was their worst nightmare coming true before his eyes.

''Your objection is noted, but I'll allow this avenue to be explored up to a point. I want to see where this goes,'' the judge said.

''Thank you, Your Honor,'' Wright said with a bright smile. ''Now, Ms. Morresey, what exactly did Trent Osborne tell you was the reason they separated?''

''Well, Maggie can't have children. She wanted to adopt. Trent wouldn't go along with her.''

''So Trenton Osborne hates children so much that he let his marriage end over it,'' Wright said at lightning speed.

''Your Honor,'' Ed said, his tone rife with disgust.

''So noted, counselor. Mr. Wright, please approach the bench.''

''I'd never say I hate kids,'' Trent whispered frantically to Ed, while the judge spoke to Wright. "That's not why I didn't want to adopt."

Ed looked at him sharply, and Trent realized that he'd just admitted that there was a solid reason behind his stand on adoption. After a long moment, Ed nodded and scribbled something on his pad. "Relax, the judge isn't happy with this guy and maybe not his clients. We have that going for us at least," he whispered. "I need a little time to think about how to counteract this mess."

The other lawyer's voice drew Trent's attention. "I'm assuming I am still allowed to explore the Osbornes' relationship, since it will so directly affect these innocent children?"

The judge nodded.

"Why would you say this miraculous reconciliation took place?"

"Calls for a conclusion, Your Honor. Ms. Morresey has no idea why they reconciled," Ed objected. "No matter what Trent Osborne might have given as a reason, he could merely have been trying to let her down easily because she had too great an expectation of where their social acquaintanceship was leading."

"So noted, counselor. Sustained."

"In that case, that's all I have for this witness," Wright said.

Ed stood, pad in hand, studying his scribble, while the other lawyer took his seat. "Now, Ms. Morresey, suppose you define for the court what you meant when you said that you and Trent Osborne were friends."

She looked into her lap, then up at the judge. "I meant friends. We confided in each other."

Ed was almost comically incredulous. "Nothing untoward, as counsel for the plaintiffs implied?"

Nadine fidgeted. "Well, no. Nothing like that at all."

Trent breathed a sigh, but still wondered why Nadine agreed to testify to help his parents. They were strangers to her. Weren't they?

"Didn't you, in fact, only attend social functions, dinners and the occasional movie or stage play with him? Didn't his work schedule at the very least prevent more contact than that?"

"Yes, those are the kind of dates he took me on, and Trent works very hard."

Ed raked his hand through his hair and sighed. "Okay. Now just to clarify things for Her Honor. Is it not true that Trent Osborne has never been inside your home? That you were only in his once? And on that occasion you arrived unannounced to see Maggie?"

"Yes. We talked a lot after that," she added, obviously recovering from the shock of Wright's badgering.

"You *talked* a lot. Went to dinner. Movies. Plays. You were at no time intimate with him, as Mr. Wright implied?"

"No. We were not!" she said, glaring at the plaintiff's lawyer.

"Mr. Wright also implied that Trent had led you to believe he intended to marry you. Did he?"

"No. I-I'm afraid that was all on my side. When

he didn't go back to Maggie after the first time she asked, I sort of started hoping.''

"It would be fair to say these hopes were one-sided, wouldn't it?''

"Yes."

"Did Mr. Osborne tell you he *hated* children? Or did he merely say he didn't believe in adoption?''

"Yes. He never said he hated children. He just said that they broke up over adoption.''

"So, all you know is that the Osbornes were having some sort of a dispute about adoption.''

"Yes!" Nadine said with a sigh.

"Nothing else, Your Honor," Ed said, a little triumph in his tone.

"Redirect, Mr. Wright?" Golden asked.

The other lawyer shook his head. "No, Your Honor."

"What now?" Trent asked, frantic.

"I'm thinking," Ed whispered.

"Your Honor, I'd like to call Trenton Osborne," Wright said. "I'd like to treat him as a hostile witness."

Trent's heart shuddered. He looked at Ed, who was pushing himself lazily to his feet. "Your Honor. This is ridiculous. Hostile witnesses in family court? Trent will be glad to testify. He already intends to. We're all supposed to be here looking after the best interests of the Osborne children.''

"I couldn't agree more, Mr. Hanson. Very well, Mr. Wright, you may question Trenton Osborne now, but be careful. You may not badger the witness. I assume you remember the definition of *badger*.''

"It's okay," Trent heard Maggie whisper past the buzzing in his ears.

"Your Honor, I would like a second or two to confer with my clients."

"A second or two? I think we can accommodate that," the judge said, looking at her watch.

Ed sat down. "One-word answers if at all possible. Don't volunteer anything."

"One-word answers," Trent repeated, then he turned to Maggie. "I'm sorry, Mag."

Maggie squeezed his forearm. "Don't be so pessimistic. The Lord's got it covered. I promise. Just tell the truth."

Trent stood, and seconds later was swearing to tell the truth with his hand on the book Maggie put so much store in. He looked over at her, and she smiled reassuringly. He thought it was ironic that she'd been worried about being the weak link in their case, and it had turned out to be him.

"Did you tell Ms. Morresey that you'd refused to adopt for five years and that your wife left over your unreasonable stand?"

"Your Honor," Ed said, "the use of the word *unreasonable* is rather inflammatory."

"Consider it ignored," the judge said, sounding annoyed. "Mr. Osborne?"

Trent glanced at Maggie. He didn't remember, but he must have told her exactly that. "Yes," he answered.

"And had you any intention of taking your wife back until your brother died?"

"No," Trent said through gritted teeth.

''No more questions,'' Wright said, and sat down.

Trent blinked. *That was it? Was the case going so badly that Wright didn't think he needed to push him, after all?*

In a fog, Trent stood and returned to his place. He felt sick to his stomach and his skin was clammy. They were going to lose the kids. And it was all his fault.

''...call Royce Osborne to the stand,'' Wright was saying when Trent managed to focus on the proceedings again. Royce looked much less like a grandfather than a potential father. He approached the stand with a confident spring in his step, his hair nowhere near as gray as it had been at their last meeting in Florida. Had he actually dyed his hair to appear younger?

Wright questioned him about his plans for the children and the adjustments he and his wife were willing to make to accommodate them. He asked about Mike. Royce spoke fondly of how hard Mike had worked to become a success. Trent felt Maggie take his hand and unfold it out of its clenched fist, and he knew she was remembering the remark one of his parents had made about Mike having been an auto mechanic. Royce mentioned that his son had become involved in a fanatical church, and added that Trent and Maggie were now being sucked in by the same cult. Ed, meanwhile, scribbled furiously.

Then the questions turned to the subject of Trent. His father said Trent had been distant as a boy, never returning the love his parents gave freely. An image of his mother pushing him away when he'd mussed her hair with an enthusiastic little-boy hug pierced Trent's heart all over again.

The pressure of Maggie's grip on his hand pulled him out of his painful remembrance because it was suddenly uncomfortably tight. Trent twisted in his seat to look at her and was surprised to see love and fury in her usually serene eyes. Lifting their clasped hands to his lips, he kissed her fingers. "Thank you," he mouthed, touched beyond measure that she would be angry for him when he was probably going to be the reason she lost the children she'd come to love as her own. He looked away from the love in her eyes, afraid he'd soon see it fade if things got worse.

Ed, he noticed, was still jotting down the odd word to trigger his memory during cross-examination. Then he surprised Trent by reserving the right to question Royce later. The judge called a fifteen-minute recess and left the bench.

"He looked too good up there," Ed said during the short break. "We've still got our side of him as a father to tell, but I wanted him off the stand. Your mother's next. No matter what she says, we have that letter she sent to Sarah. That has to make her look pretty bad."

When court resumed, Trent stared down at the table, then closed his eyes as his mother walked forward. *Please, Jesus. If You're real. If You really do intervene in people's lives, let us keep the kids. Tell me what You want me to do to make it right and I'll do it.*

Maggie watched as Albertine settled into the witness chair. She still had faith that everything would turn out fine, but she was angry for Trent's sake. Albertine looked cool in an ice-blue suit, her blond hair in a youthful style that took years off her looks. She smiled sweetly and made all the appropriate declarations about her good intentions. She told the judge that she only wanted a chance to give her beloved grandchildren a wonderful life, and that Trent and Maggie would be welcome to see them occasionally if their marriage survived. She expressed worry that the children were being brought up in an unhealthy environment with guardians who had just recently been estranged to the point of divorce. Albertine also blamed Trent and Maggie for the estrangement from Michael that had kept the elder Osbornes from knowing the children. That was something she said she wanted desperately to change.

"Your witness, counselor," Wright said with a smug smile directed at all three of them. Maggie wished the judge had been able to see the gesture. Maybe it would make her as mad as it did Maggie.

"Oh, I'm going to eat this guy for lunch," Ed muttered as he stood.

"Aren't you concerned about the impact four children will have on your social life, Mrs. Osborne?" Ed asked.

"There'll be changes, of course," she said with a beatific smile. "But the sacrifice will be worth it. Children are our future, after all."

"So the number of children doesn't worry you at all."

"We intend to hire a full-time nanny to help out,

but the day-to-day rearing will be our responsibility. Bedtimes. Playing in the yard. That sort of thing.''

She smiled, and Maggie wondered how long she'd practiced looking so loving.

"We've already installed playground equipment for them. Money is no object for us, after all. The children will attend all the best schools and have every advantage we can give them.''

Ed turned away and returned to the table. "Are you saying that you can do more financially for them than my clients?''

"We are more established than my son could possibly be at his age.''

"Your Honor, both the elder Osbornes have mentioned their financial position as if it were an issue here. I'd like to place into evidence the financial statement of Trent and Maggie Osborne. To summarize, it shows that they have every resource available to them that Royce Osborne has. Plus, they have youth on their side.''

Then he handed Albertine the letter. "Mrs. Osborne, do you recognize this letter?''

She went a little pale, then she nodded and said, "Yes.'' But she quickly shook off her shock, sat a little straighter, visibly pulling herself together.

"Is that your handwriting all the way through?'' Ed asked.

"Ahem. Yes. Yes, it is.''

Ed reached out for it and for a second Albertine resisted returning it to the lawyer. "I'd like to place this into evidence, as well. Would you like to sum-

marize the note for the court?'' Ed asked Trent's
mother.

''It was a letter I sent my daughter-in-law. But you
have to understand,'' she said, turning to speak directly to the judge, ''Sarah just kept having children.
My son was incapable of handling that much responsibility. He was special, you see, Your Honor. He
worked hard, as my husband mentioned, but at a me-
nial job. He was slow, and Sarah took advantage of
him from the beginning.''

''You didn't approve of your daughter-in-law, did
you? Didn't you, in fact, try to buy Sarah out of
Mike's life?''

''Your Honor,'' Wright called out. ''What does
Mrs. Osborne's opinion of her late daughter-in-law
have to do with this matter?''

''I allowed you to explore the near breakup of the
current custodial parents' marriage. I think we can
indulge counsel in this.''

''Did you try to pay Sarah to drop out of Michael's
life?'' Ed asked again.

''She knew we had money. She saw him as a meal
ticket.''

''Is that a yes, Mrs. Osborne?''

''Yes!''

Ed picked up the letter. ''Back to the number of
children you want the court to place in your care. Do
you recognize the phrase 'Only dogs have more than
two children'?''

''I was trying to shock some sense into her. She
was dragging my son down. They were living in a
wreck of a home that we'd heard he had to spend

every waking hour trying to repair. She had no business increasing his burden. But that has nothing to do with the children. They are all still precious parts of him—Michael, I mean.''

"I thought she saw him as a meal ticket? Yet, we know she had his four children and lived with him and them in what you yourself just called a wreck of a house."

"In the beginning she must have thought we would continue to support him."

"But you weren't supporting him by the time they married. Michael no longer lived in your house by then, did he?"

"No."

"Michael, the son you describe as *slow*, owned a successful foreign car repair business that was profiting him over a hundred-thousand dollars a year by the time of his death. When was the last time you even saw your son, Mrs Osborne?"

"Several years ago, I'm afraid. Michael misunderstood what we tried to do to protect him from Sarah. We attended his wedding, but Trent and Maggie had painted us in the worst possible light by then. Michael always listened to Trent."

Ed approached the table where Maggie and Trent sat. Trent leaned forward and signaled to him. Ed bent over and listened as Trent whispered in his ear. With a scowl, and without turning around to face the judge, Ed said, "No more questions at this time, Your Honor."

"The plaintiff rests," the other lawyer called out.

Ed schooled his features into a bland mask and

turned to face Judge Golden. "A short recess, Your Honor?"

The judge checked her watch. "Let's do an hour for lunch. Then you can present your case, Mr. Hanson."

The judge left, and Ed turned to them. "What's this all about, Trent?"

"You're still going to need the kids and Nancy, aren't you?" Trent asked. He knew his tone clearly showed the strain this was having on him.

Ed nodded. "I still have all of Michael's records to present to show that he was indeed in full control of his life and faculties and that your parents were way off-base about you and Sarah controlling him. But I won't guarantee anything. I think it's better to err on the side of caution, so we're going to have to bring the kids in. Your parents are just so darn cool under fire. They've thought of a noble explanation for every rotten trick they've pulled over the years. I think the judge may see through them, but I can't be sure. And I don't want to chance it."

"Put me back on the stand after you give her all the paperwork. I don't want those kids exposed to this, or those two sitting there looking so sure of themselves. That'll scare them to death, and I'm worried about the strain on Nancy, too. Suppose she has another heart attack over this. The kids have lost enough."

"You'll get your chance. You need to give some explanation of the adoption thing. But Trent, we're still going to have to call Mickey and Rachel."

Trent turned to her. "Mag, take the kids to lunch.

Ed and I need to talk. I'll see you back here when court reconvenes.''

"Talk? Talk about what?" she asked.

"You'll see. Don't you worry. They aren't going to get our kids. Please, go to lunch. I won't be able to do this any other way. And I know now what I have to do. It's way past time. Ed?" Trent stood and walked out of the courtroom.

Looking more than slightly rattled, Ed gathered his papers and followed Trent up the aisle.

Maggie just stared after them, wondering what on earth was going on.

Chapter Sixteen

The hour lunch break with the children went quickly and served to turn up any latent jittery nerves Maggie had about the custody suit. She found it was easier to tell others that they could trust in the Lord, than it was to do it one hundred percent of the time herself. Doubts seemed to creep in at the worst of times. And seeing the children—youngest to oldest—frightened by the tension they sensed in the adults in their lives and by the strange surroundings had undone some of her confidence. She was worried. Suppose it was part of the Lord's far-reaching plan to let the children go to their grandparents…

Maggie knew that with the Lord's help she would survive but Trent didn't have the Lord to rely on. She tried to pray for him and for her own restored peace while walking back to the courtroom, but an image of the way he'd looked at her before leaving kept intruding. His had been an expression full of loss and grim resolve. What was he up to?

She walked into the courtroom alone to find that Trent wasn't there yet, but Ed was. So were her in-laws, who shot her twin venomous looks.

"Where is Trent and what's going on?" she asked Ed.

"I'm not at liberty to say, but Trent will be here in a minute." Ed didn't look at her, but continued to scratch out words and rewrite them on his ever-present yellow legal pad.

Maggie sat down, and seconds later Trent strode in, a look of iron-willed determination on his face. If he'd timed it any closer, he would have been late—and now they had no time to talk. Maggie wondered if he'd planned it that way, because the judge entered just as he reached his seat.

"Is the defense ready?" Judge Golden asked.

Ed, looking strained, glanced at Trent.

Trent nodded sharply and clenched his jaw even more tightly. "Let's end this now," he said grimly.

"Yes, we're ready to proceed, Your Honor. First, as Michael and Sarah are not present to set the record straight, I would like to place in evidence several more documents. Michael's school records showing clearly that he was an intelligent child who was severely learning disabled—a disability that was pointed out to his parents when he was in fourth grade. All help for him was rejected by his parents—"

"Objection, Your Honor!" Wright shouted.

"Counsel is well within his rights to refute testi-

mony presented by the plaintiff. Although I have yet
to understand why she did so, it was your client who
introduced her son's intellect into the record.''

"I think I can answer that with my next document," Ed said as the other attorney sat back down,
looking disgruntled. "The wills of Sarah and Michael
in which Trent and Maggie Osborne are named guardians of the children. You will see a letter expressing
their wish that Michael's parents be kept out of their
children's lives. By making my late client appear to
have been unduly influenced by his older brother and
unable to make these sorts of decisions for himself,
this document would lose all impact.

"Which brings me to the other two documents."
Ed sighed. "I had hoped to avoid using this avenue
of defense, but I know Michael would want his in-
structions for his children taken seriously by the court.
What I hope Your Honor will see here is evidence of
the skewed view Royce and Albertine Osborne have
always taken of those less highly placed on the social
scale—like Sarah Merritt. It was this influence that
Michael feared most for his children. Authenticated
by the District Attorney and notarized as such, I give
you Michael Osborne's arrest record, both juvenile
and adult—possession of a controlled substance, DUI,
resisting arrest. As you see, I could go on but there's
no need, because you will also note that there are no
more arrests after the date of the second document—
Trent and Maggie Osborne's marriage license. Less
than a week later, Michael met Sarah Merritt and her
influence began to change his life. So, yes, Sarah
greatly influenced Michael, but it was an influence

that turned him from an angry, misdirected young man into a respected citizen of this county.''

The judge accepted all the documents with a nod. ''Do you intend to call witnesses?''

''Trenton Osborne,'' Ed said.

Trent stood and walked stiffly to the witness chair, his demeanor quite different from his earlier panic when called by Jason Wright. This was the Trent who had successfully built and run a high-tech firm in a cutthroat field. It was also a Trent who looked as if he'd lost his last friend, or was about to. Maggie felt sweat break out over her entire body. Whatever he was about to reveal, she suddenly knew it would have a negative effect on their relationship.

The judge reminded Trent that he was still under oath, then Ed asked his first question. ''Your father testifed that you were a cold, unloving son. How would you characterize your parents?''

''Your Honor, I—'' the other lawyer cut in.

''Mr. Wright, I would like to get this matter settled today,'' the judge responded. ''You introduced the kind of boy Trenton Osborne was. I see no problem hearing his view of his parents at the same point in time. Answer the question, Mr. Osborne.''

''They're the ones who were cold and unloving to me. I never understood until I was twelve. I overheard them planning to send me away to boarding school. That's what my parents think is a good education. They were rarely around. We were raised by staff— a series of nannies and housekeepers. I can't believe they'll be different with Mike's kids. What hurt about being sent away was that they wanted me out of the picture because...," Trent hesitated and looked straight at his parents. "Because they were sorry they'd adopted me."

Maggie gasped, and Trent looked over at her, his aching heart reflected in his eyes. Luckily, her sharp intake of breath was drowned out by Albertine Osborne's excited flurry of words to her husband. Maggie looked over at them, seeing utter shock written in their expressions.

"Until this day you never let them know that you'd overheard them talking, did you?" Ed asked.

"No. I was afraid they'd give up all pretense that I was part of their family, and that I'd lose Mike completely. Later, well, I guess I always worried that his feelings toward me would change, so I kept silent."

"Is this why you were so against adoption?" Ed asked.

"Back then I thought that was why they didn't love me, but I've seen others adopt through the years and love their children. I realized it was they who didn't know how to love. Neither me nor Michael, who was actually their biological son. So, no, that isn't the reason. I'd actually decided against fathering children at all by the time I graduated from college. Then I met Maggie. I decided that loving her as much as I did, I could love children of that love. But no children came, and in time I started thinking that because I'd never been loved as a child, I wouldn't know how to give love to one. I didn't want to hurt children the way I'd been hurt. But we couldn't get pregnant, so I just kept my fears hidden. Then she wanted to adopt and I refused. It was an excuse—a way to run from my fear without admitting to it.''

Maggie ached for Trent. He'd borne this pain as a child alone, feeling unloved and trying to preserve the only love he'd ever known—that of his brother.

But then other thoughts occurred to her. Fine. He hadn't trusted his parents enough to tell them what he knew, but what about her? He hadn't trusted her either. And he'd had a reason, however painful, for his stand on adoption. Had he told her, they might have been able to work through their problems. But he hadn't trusted her, and he'd let his fears tear their marriage apart. He'd let her shoulder all the blame even after they'd reconciled.

As Maggie fought to keep the anger from showing on her face, the judge's voice called her back to the proceedings. ''Mr. Osborne, I'm confused,'' Judge Golden said. ''So I'm going to take the liberty of asking you a direct question. Why, if you never wanted children at all, are you fighting to keep four of them?''

Trent answered without a moment's hesitation. ''After Mike and Sarah died, I took on raising the kids because I didn't want my parents to get them. At first I was afraid that I'd scar them for life, but I was wrong. I can't imagine how much it would hurt to lose those kids. I love Mike's children as much as if they were my own.''

He shook his head. ''No, that's not quite right. Maybe I love them more because they're part of Mike. They're all I have left of him. The worst part of being sent away to school when I was a kid was losing Mike. Losing him permanently was devastating. He was a wonderful, funny, talented man. My best friend. That's how I want his children to remember him. Not slow—as if he needed a keeper. And Sarah—sweet, patient, kind Sarah. She deserves to be remembered this way and not as a gold digger, the way my parents always saw her. Because she wasn't. She loved my brother. Deeply."

The judge nodded. "Mr. Hanson, I'd like to see the children before you proceed with any further witnesses."

"But your honor," Trent protested.

Winifred Golden's slight smile to him was kind. "I'm well aware of all the pre-trial motions, and that you and your wife wanted to keep the children safely out of this. I also see that two of them are tentatively scheduled as well as their maternal grandmother. I understand and agree with your reasons for trying to protect them. I do, however, prefer to meet the children whose lives my decisions will affect. I like to find a nonthreatening way for them to have their say in where they live, if at all possible. I've seen the home studies and now I'd like to talk with them. Relax. I don't look nearly as scary without the black robes. We will reconvene in an hour."

Looking like a deer caught in the glare of headlights, Trent stared at Judge Golden when she hammered her gavel down and stood to leave. Maggie felt the same profound sense of shock descend on her. Nothing in this day had happened the way she'd thought it would. And now these revelations about Trent left her emotions stirred up and confused.

Where, she wondered, did she even start trying to unravel years of half truths in order to build a relationship with a husband she'd never really known?

But on the upside, Maggie realized that all her nervousness had dissipated. She wasn't even fazed by the thought of the interview the judge was about to conduct with the children. She was once again completely able to trust in the Lord where they were concerned. The Lord would see to it that the children remained with them. Perhaps they would walk through fire, not only in court, but also in its aftermath.

Trent walked back to the table, his heart in his throat. Maggie was furious. Maybe even beyond furious. But she'd masked it quickly for the judge's benefit. He'd watched her as closely as he could, and he'd seen the moment she'd realized that he'd let her accept all the blame for the divorce. "How angry are you?" he asked once seated.

She looked straight ahead, refusing to meet his eyes. "I don't think here is the place to get into a discussion of how angry I am. Much better done later in private and after I've had some time."

"Some time? Some time for what? To calm down? To—"

"Later means later," she said through gritted teeth, her expression a facade of neutrality.

"Can you a least tell me if you think I did the right thing? Do you think I gave us a better chance?"

"The judge seemed to be leaning our way, don't you think?" Maggie asked, leaning forward to see past him to Ed where Trent imagined she was directing her question.

"I think she may have had their number all along. I've never seen her smile before. I'm sorry, Trent. If I'd read her correctly before I let you get up there and..."

Trent nodded, still watching Maggie closely when she turned to stare at him with open fury in her brown eyes.

"In other words," she said, "if Ed had realized that we had more than a fighting chance, you wouldn't have needed to bare your soul. And I never would have known any of what you said on the stand. I guess for once I have something to thank your parents for. I'd have gone on for years, blaming myself for all of our problems every time I remembered our time apart!" Maggie stood. "I need some air," she snapped, checking her wristwatch. "I'll make sure I'm back on time."

This time it was Maggie who timed her entry back into the courtroom to perfection. She no sooner resumed her seat than Judge Golden returned.

"All rise," the bailiff said, and called the court to order.

"As I said earlier, I want to get this over with," Judge Golden began. "Will counsel please approach the bench."

Trent longed to grasp hold of Maggie's hand, but he knew he was on his own. He hoped not forever. Elbows on the table, he clasped his hands together and leaned his chin atop his knuckles. Ed Hanson nodded repeatedly as did Wright. *Please God. Please let this be good,* he begged the God he'd been turning to more and more often these days.

Ed pivoted toward them, his face impassive as he returned to their table.

"Mr. Wright, have you anything to add on summation?" Judge Golden asked.

Wright took a few steps backward and waxed poetic for several minutes about his clients, their pain, their good intentions and their ability to carry them to fruition.

Trent, meanwhile, saw Ed begin to once again scribble notes furiously. "What's going on? Isn't she going to let you call Maggie? Aren't you going to object?"

Ed shielded his mouth with his hand. "Not yet," he whispered. "I don't think it's necessary. I think we've won. If not, she's given us the perfect opening for an appeal."

"Thank you, Mr. Wright," Golden said, when Wright took his seat. "I've never been particularly fond of the idea of keeping grandparents from seeing their grandchildren, and I often order visitation. I have even terminated parental rights in favor of those of grandparents for the good of the children. But this isn't going to be one of those cases.

"I was quite frankly appalled that this case was scheduled for two days before Christmas. I began to have a little hope for the children when Mr. Hanson tried to block the children's involvement or at least limit their involvement.

"I purposely observed the children being dropped off by Trent and Maggie Osborne this morning. I saw the obvious love and attachment between the children and them. I came in here this morning wondering what kind of people would try to rip a bond like that apart.

"Then I encountered the elder Osbornes here in my court. I listened to their opinions on child-rearing, then saw evidence that they had done a great disservice to their own children over the years."

She looked directly at Trent and Maggie for the first time and smiled. "I hereby grant permanent custody to Trenton and Margaret Osborne. I would like to suggest that you consider formally adopting the children. It would go a long way toward making them feel secure. Furthermore, after talking to the two oldest children, I leave to your discretion any future contact with the paternal grandparents. Have a good Christmas. You have four lovely children. Now go home and enjoy them. Court is adjourned."

Chapter Seventeen

"Let's go tell the children and get them out of here," Maggie said.

"Yeah. And maybe we could go out for an early dinner to celebrate," Trent tried, hoping to put off their inevitable confrontation a little longer.

Maggie shook her head and stood. "Grace is going to be really cranky by now, and I wouldn't count on Daniel being any better after being cooped up in one room almost all day. I think take-out pizza is about as much celebration as we're likely to have."

Trent pushed himself to his feet. Their victory had left him relieved, but not at all lighthearted. Instead, he felt weighed down by fears of losing Maggie. He'd been wrong to let her shoulder the blame for their breakup alone, and now he hadn't a clue how to make reparation.

As he walked into the hall behind Maggie and Ed,

Trent heard his name. He turned, and came face to face with Nadine Morresey.

"Hello," she said, including Maggie in the greeting.

"Trent, I'll go on ahead and get the children. Hello, Nadine. Sorry you were dragged into this," Maggie said, and walked away.

Trent watched her go, wondering at her grace. Most women would have verbally cut Nadine off at the knees. "I really have nothing to say to you," he told Nadine, and turned to follow Maggie.

Nadine grasped the sleeve of his topcoat. "No, I'm sure you don't. But I needed to explain. Trent, I honestly thought I was helping you or I never would have agreed to testify. I was as shocked by Mr. Wright's line of questioning as you were."

Trent stared at her. She had seemed shocked. And embarrassed. "We could have lost those kids to my parents thanks to you."

"But that's just it. I thought that's what you wanted. As far as I knew, your going back to Maggie was nothing more than a noble gesture. You said you wanted to be free of Maggie. I certainly never thought you wanted your brother's children—not after you let your marriage break up over adoption. I care very much for you, Trent. And your parents assured me that you'd be grateful for my intervention. I also thought they wanted what was best for you. Your mother said she was worried that Maggie was dragging you into something you couldn't handle. Then I heard you'd sold CSD to stay home and renovate the house. Now I see that she encouraged me all along after Maggie left you.''

Trent suddenly recalled something that had happened that day after the accident when his parents showed up at the hospital. His mother had said something about Maggie's visit to his office but had stopped before completing the thought. She could only have known that Maggie had come to see him if someone had told her about the visit. Oh, now he understood that incident, and a whole lot more. Trent frowned, remembering Nadine's arrival. The doorbell had rung and he'd hobbled stiffly to the door to find Nadine in the hall. She'd asked if Maggie were home and apologized for stopping without calling first. She'd been in the neighborhood. Had her surprise that Maggie had left him been convincing, or had his medication-fogged mind just seen what he'd been expecting to see?

''The night I hurt my back, was that little drop-in visit to Maggie a setup?'' he asked her.

''No. Oh, I was afraid you'd think that. I didn't know about your separation before I stopped by that night. But when I saw you so hurt and alone, my heart went out to you. I couldn't understand why Maggie would choose raising a stranger's child over standing by so wonderful a man.''

Trent ignored the compliment. ''So how did my mother get into the picture?''

''We're both on the same hospital committee. I mentioned that you and I had had dinner a few times. She encouraged me where you were concerned. I see now that she was serving her own purpose. I'm sorry

I listened to her. I'm especially sorry about trying to save you from yourself this morning. If it makes you feel any better, I think your mother truly believes you would have been better off. Please, tell Maggie I'm sorry."

After Nadine left, Trent shoved his hands in his pants pockets and leaned back against the marble wall. He stared unseeing at the floor. He was so deep in thought that he didn't realize anyone had approached until a pair of oxblood wing tips stepped into view. Trent looked up straight into his father's cool blue eyes.

"Trent," the older man said, "we know you needn't do as we ask, but Michael was our son. We'd like to see his children occasionally."

Trent's first reaction was to argue but something made him hold back. Maggie's influence? Jim Dillon's? God's? He didn't know. "Mickey, Rachel and Daniel were badly frightened by the prospect of having to leave us. And to all of them, you're virtual strangers. Maggie and I can't in good conscience answer your question until they've settled down. And even then, if we agreed it would be a supervised visit."

"I see," Royce said stiffly.

"I really don't think you do, Father, or supervision wouldn't be necessary." Eyes narrowed in thought, Trent considered his father. "Tell me, why all this sudden interest in these kids? You let Michael slip out of your lives years ago. You could have apologized after the wedding. What did you think his invitation to attend his wedding was if not an olive branch? Believe me, it wasn't some shallow attempt to not air the family's dirty linen. If that's what you thought, you didn't know Mike at all.''

Unnoticed, Albertine had approached and now stood at her husband's side, facing Trent. She nodded. ''You may be right, but we can't change the past or see Michael again to apologize. I am sorry the children were scared. We didn't think of this as particularly frightening to them. We just wanted a chance to do better by his children than we did by Michael. We would have done better this time. I know we would have. We failed you both so miserably.''

''You failed us because you didn't know how to love us. Neither of you know what love is. What I've never been able to understand is why you adopted me when you never wanted me in the first place.''

His mother blinked, clearly shocked by his questions. ''Not want you? We *chose* you.''

''What happened—you wanted children until you had them? You practically let the staff raise us. Sending me away to Ruxley was just another stage of being ignored. And it certainly came in handy to hide the adopted son far from home where no one would be able to compare your two children.''

''I told you then,'' his father said, ''it was an honor to go to Ruxley. *I* went there. My own son didn't get to go there.''

''You forget I overheard what you two said the night you discussed what to do with me. You were never able to forget that I wasn't really your son, were you?'' Trent asked, and wasn't at all surprised when

Royce turned and walked away without answering. And that was answer enough.

Albertine hesitated to follow, and Trent found himself blurting out the question that had haunted him for twenty-four years. "Why didn't my real mother want me?" he asked her as she watched her husband move away. Then after closing her eyes, she took a deep breath and looked back up at Trent. "They told us at the agency to tell you the truth, but Royce didn't want you to know. He's very proud of all you've accomplished and has always been proud to call you his son.

"Your biological parents didn't have a choice about giving you up for adoption. It wasn't a case of them not wanting you, and I'm sorry you've thought that. It's one of life's ironies, really. An auto accident took our second son out of our lives years after one brought our first son to us. You see, your parents were in an auto crash, and your father, James, died almost immediately. Your mother, Kathleen, lived long enough to deliver you. She named you Trenton, knowing you would go to someone else to raise and that you'd at least still have their last name. Trenton was their surname. We decided to have you keep the name in honor of her last request. No family could be traced for them, but I have pictures of them together that were found in their wallets. I'll see you get them."

Stunned, Trent never realized she turned to walk away until he heard the *tap-tap* of her high heels on the hard floor. "Mother," he called.

Albertine looked back.

"Thank you. Thank you for telling me about them."

His mother nodded and walked away. She looked suddenly older, and not so much like a wicked woman as she did a sad misguided soul.

What's real, and what did I imagine? Did I base my entire life on lies? He turned and saw Maggie coming down the hall with the children, and had to wonder the same thing. *What's real, and what did I imagine? Is there a chance she could forgive me? Still love me?*

"Daddy!" Rachel's voice echoed in the hall, pulling Trent away from useless speculation. There was joy in the *pitter-patter* of her Mary Janes on the terrazzo tile. He bent down just in time to catch her up in his arms, then he swung her high. Her arms wrapped around his neck, hugging him for all he was worth.

"The nice lady said we were going to be yours forever and ever," Rachel told him in a rush. "And Aunt Maggie says she's right!"

Trent felt a smile tip his lips in spite of the problems between him and Maggie. "She did, did she?"

Rachel's nod was enthusiastic, her red-gold ponytail bobbing with each movement. "And the nice lady said we didn't have to go anywhere we didn't want to go. Daniel said he didn't want to go to school anymore on show-and-tell day. But she said school didn't count and that he should be a lawyer when he grows up and be Uncle Ed's pardner. But Daniel told her he was your pardner 'cause you always call him 'pardner.'"

"It sounds like you had a long talk with the judge."

"Oh, she wasn't a judge. She was Winnie. She said to call her Winnie." Rachel frowned, clearly considering something intently. "She knew an awful lot about us. Maybe she was a Christmas angel!"

Trent chuckled. "Well, she was sure our angel today. Winnie gave us all a happy Christmas this year, sweetheart." He set Rachel down. As he was straightening, he came face to face with Maggie, who had Grace in her arms.

"Here, let me take her. She's quite an armful, aren't you, munchkin?" he asked Grace, putting his arms out to the toddler. Grace had other ideas and clung to Maggie, burying her head against Maggie's neck. "Uh-oh. Somebody's really had it."

It was obvious from the look in Maggie's eyes that her anger hadn't cooled a bit. "Mom and Nancy went ahead to the van. I thought you would have followed me. What did Nadine have to say that took so long?"

Trent wondered if reading a little jealousy into her question wasn't hoping for too much. "Apparently, she appeared in court today to help my parents stop me from making a noble sacrifice. I don't know if I can forgive her even though my mother manipulated her shamefully. I didn't even bother to confront my parents about recruiting her for today, though. They approached me about the children."

"What about them?"

Trent shook his head. "No threats. They want to see the kids. I was noncommittal. I said we couldn't even think about it until the kids have calmed down.

Apparently, my mother hadn't considered that they might be upset by all this. She said some other things I'll tell you about later, if you're interested."

Maggie gave a sharp nod. "Oh, we'll talk later," she told him with fire in her brown eyes.

It was not so much a promise as a threat.

Maggie buckled Grace into her car seat and closed the door. She had to get a hold on her anger before the children or the moms caught on that all was not joy and jubilation between her and Trent. Going out to dinner as Trent had suggested started looking better and better in the small confines of the van. With so many others to talk to and so many distractions, she might be able to distance herself from him and what he'd done. She just might get through the time until the children went to bed without giving in to the urge to scream or the need to cry. The two urges traded places in her heart every two minutes.

"How long would you say it would take to get to Springfield?" she asked Trent as she buckled her seat belt.

He started as if shocked to hear her address him at all. "A-about forty-five minutes," Trent replied. "Why?"

"I thought about your suggestion. Grace is already dropping off to sleep, and Daniel won't be far behind. With a forty- or forty-five-minute nap they should be able to handle a celebration. How about Klaus Mouse's Pizza House?"

"Klaus Mouse?" Trent looked so doubtful that she

almost laughed but somehow she maintained a neutral tone.

"He's a big mechanical mouse dressed in lederhosen. He and his other mechanical friends do a stage show. They sing and play instruments. Klaus does a stand-up comedy routine for children, and I hear his girlfriend even dances while they play."

"I'll bet the kids will love it. This is their celebration, after all." Trent grinned, but Maggie saw fear in his eyes. And she was taken aback by that fear, not understanding it at all. Then he reached for her hand and whispered something that explained so much and fed her fury even more. "Please don't leave me over this, Mag. I'll find a way to make it up to you if it takes my last breath."

Maggie gaped at him. He thought she planned to leave him again!

With her mother and Nancy Merritt along, and the distraction of the crazy-looking giant puppets entertaining the children, Maggie managed to get through the rest of the day without blowing a gasket. Before Trent had taken the stand in their defense, Maggie knew she would have blamed herself for Trent's lack of trust. But no more. She'd come to realize that he had still not learned to trust her to stand by him.

Maggie closed Grace's door with the final goodnight of the evening and went to the big bathroom the children shared. After their baths it was a mess of splashed water and haphazardly strewn clothes. Normally she had them help, but they'd been so tired after their emotional day that she'd just steered them all to bed. Trent had made himself scarce after they'd all returned home, saying he had things to do in his workshop.

She knew he'd planned to build each child a unique gift from Santa. She assumed the gifts were not quite finished, but now that he'd missed the children's bedtime, she had to wonder if he was hiding from her. Well, she thought as she tossed the last errant sock into the hamper, if that was what he was up to, he was in for a shock.

She stalked to the phone and called Claire. "Hi, I saw your lights over there. I hope you weren't busy packing to go to your son's tomorrow," she said when Claire answered.

"I packed two days ago, dear. Do you need something?"

"Actually I do. I wondered if it would be too much of an imposition for you to come over and watch the children for a little while. They're all in bed, and Trent's out working in the shop."

"You either have some last-minute shopping to do or you want to get in on the fun down there in Santa's workshop."

If Claire thought that, Maggie decided, one really furious wife had just missed her chance for an Oscar. "I'm headed to the shop. Could you come over?"

"I'll be right there."

Maggie tossed a coat over her shoulders and met Claire on the porch. "Thanks. Help yourself to some cookies. Water's on for tea or instant cocoa. See you in a while."

"Take your time, dear. Your Trent's tall for an elf,

but he's got the job down pat. It looks like a lot of fun's going on down there.''

Maggie unlocked the door to ''Santa's Workshop'' and entered quietly. The smell of polyurethane, oil stain and freshly cut wood hung in the air. Trent had Christmas carols blaring on a small radio. At first she didn't see him but then she noticed the sole of his shoe sticking out into the aisle on the other side of the table saw.

She walked over, and he looked up, startled. She arched her eyebrow. ''Hiding?'' she asked as she reached over and snapped off the music.

Trent bristled and stood. ''No. I have a lot to get done before tomorrow night.''

Maggie crossed her arms and leaned back against the table saw. ''You'll have to take a few minutes off, because we need to talk.''

Trent turned away. Wiping his hands, he let out a soul-deep sigh. ''All right. I was hiding. I don't want to hear what I think you're about to say.''

''You don't have a clue what I'm going to say!'' she shouted.

Trent whirled, clearly shocked at her tone. ''Of course I do. I know how angry you are.'' He held a hand out to her. ''Please. I'm sorry. I don't know what else to say. I told you in the car that I'd make it up to you. And I will, if you just give me a chance to figure out how.''

''You don't know,'' Maggie said, despair clawing at her heart with sharp talons. ''You don't know a thing about how I feel or why I feel the way I do. I need answers, Trent. I need to know why you just stood back and let me flog myself daily for leaving you when you could have prevented it in the first place."

"I let you leave because I saw how much not having children hurt you. I was hurt that you left. Devastated, believe me. But I was relieved, too, because I thought you would be able to go on with your life and have the children I'd denied you."

"And it never occurred to you to tell me why you didn't want to adopt? What am I saying? Why you didn't want any children at all? And now that I think about it, you were only minimally cooperative with the fertility doctor, too. All it would have taken was five minutes of honest conversation to help me understand."

"I couldn't tell you. I was afraid you'd leave."

"So you dangled an artificial carrot in front of me for almost eight years! First, it was that we'd have children after I'd established my career and you had yours on solid ground. Then a year of trying on our own to conceive, then three years of fertility doctors. All the while you were secretly hoping we'd fail. Then there was a full year of arguments and anguish while I had to watch us grow farther and farther apart. And all the time you knew why. You had a choice but I was just along for the ride."

Trent raked a hand agitatedly through his thick black hair. "I know! Don't you think I know? You think I haven't said as much to myself? I just couldn't bring myself to tell you."

"And do you know why?" Maggie demanded. "Because you never trusted me. I didn't destroy your trust. You never had any in me in the first place. Before we ever had problems, back when you apparently thought you wanted children—before we were even married—you didn't trust me with what was the defining fact of your life. Your adoption. Why Trent? Why could you never trust me?''

She could see that there was an answer. And that he knew what it was. She could, but something held him back. Eyes eternally sad, Trent shook his head.

"Tell me, do you love me at all?"

"Of course I do!" he protested immediately—vehemently.

"Or," she continued as if he hadn't spoken, "do you just like the idea of being loved by me? What do you want from this marriage, Trent? Because I'm telling you right now, I'm not leaving. And—" she stepped toe-to-toe with him and poked his chest with her index finger "—you'd better never ask me again if I'm going to, if you know what's good for you! So you just think about that. Because, buster, you've got a marriage whether you want one or not! It's up to you what kind you want to have."

She pivoted and stormed out. The cold December night made her quickly aware that her cheeks were flushed. She couldn't face Claire like that so she walked to the street down Paradise Found's long private drive, then back again before entering the house.

After good-nights to Claire and a soothing cup of herbal tea, Maggie went to bed and was surprised to feel herself drifting toward sleep. She never heard Trent come to bed, and she only knew he had because his side of the bed had been disturbed when she woke at seven the next morning to Grace's usual call for freedom from her crib. He was already gone, back to the workshop, and all that Christmas Eve day was a repeat of the night before. He came in for meals, then quietly excused himself to work on gifts. Was he hiding? Thinking about their future? She didn't know, but she wished she did.

Chapter Eighteen

It was the hour before dawn that saw Trent putting the last gift under the tree. The girls had both asked for cradles and high chairs, and Rachel had asked for a toy kitchen sink and stove. And he'd built every last one of them, plus a table and chairs set that he'd fashioned like a breakfast nook.

Trent smiled, thinking of the two girls sharing tea parties with their dolls; maybe even their brothers, too. He'd already checked out a third-floor room he was going to fix up for the girls as a playroom. They'd have a regular little apartment up there by the time he got through.

He'd earmarked another room to fix up for the rough-and-tumble boys. He chuckled. Soundproofing would probably play a large role in that project.

Against the far wall of the living room now stood a four-year-old's version of a computer table. It was all ready for the child's version of a computer that

Daniel had been coveting since being exposed to one while visiting Mickey at Shriners Hospital. A red wagon, its red paint finally dry, waited for him to hitch it to his Big Wheel, as well.

Mickey, who was as mechanically inclined as his father, had been tougher to plan for because he'd asked for nothing that Trent could build. Trent had decided on a wooden toolbox, which he'd filled with smaller tools that were just the right size for small hands and a tool bench that had adjustable legs so it would grow with the boy. He'd found plans for some wooden games and a couple of other projects, and had made a good start on them so that Mickey could finish with his new tools.

Each gift sported a tag that read *From Santa*.

Maggie had apparently already put out the gifts the two of them had bought at local toy stores to give to the children. They were all gaily wrapped and be-ribboned, and stacked in a riot of colors and shapes.

Trent knew that inside the biggest boxes were the computer for Daniel and a little pink-and-blue copy of Daniel's Big Wheel for Grace. Under the big tree were baby dolls and baby doll clothes for the girls. And there were pots, pans, dishes and flatware along with pretend boxes and cans of food. The kitchen he'd built in miniature was going to be as well-equipped as a real one.

Of course, Maggie didn't know how crazy he'd gone with the little kitchen. It not only had a stove and sink but a refrigerator and a breakfront to match the table and chairs. It had everything the family kitchen had. He'd gone overboard and done all he could think of, trying to make this Christmas perfect, hoping to overshadow the tension that had only lessened with Judge Golden's ruling.

He straightened the bow on the computer table and stepped back to look around. The living room was the perfect picture of the night before Christmas, with the tree lights reflecting off gifts and packages and candles glowing brightly in the windows. Snow had even begun to fall sometime in the last hour, and now it coated the ground and trees. It *should* have been perfect. But there was still a place so empty and hollow inside him that he wanted to sit down and cry like a baby.

He wished that, just as in the old poem, Saint Nick would appear at the fireplace and tell him he had nothing to dread. But Trent knew he did.

He was losing Maggie again, even if she didn't intend to leave him. He was losing her love and all the closeness they'd built between them these last months. He was losing her because there was something wrong with him that he just couldn't define, and so he was powerless to fix it.

And he really didn't know how to explain it to her. How could he make her understand why he'd been so afraid to be himself with her, when to all outward appearances the world at large saw him as a success in life?

Weary beyond the all-nighter he'd just put in finishing the toys, Trent trudged up the stairs and stumbled into the bathroom to shower off the sawdust. Then, practically asleep on his feet, he dropped down so hard onto the bed that he bounced Maggie awake.

She sat up, pushed the hair off her face and looked toward the dawn sky. "Tell me you aren't just coming to bed."

Trent yawned. "Wish I could, but guilty as charged. All the toys are done, though. I think maybe I went a little crazy. There's hardly any room to move in the living room."

"The kids will be thrilled. You'd better get some sleep. Christmas mornings come early if I remember correctly."

Trent yawned again and flopped back in bed. "Yeah. I sure better—"

"Mama! Ma! Daddy! Daddy! Grace get up now. Criksmus! It Criksmus!" Grace bellowed.

Trent opened one eye and turned toward Maggie. "Please. Tell me I didn't hear that!"

"Would that I could, Daddy. What is it? Six o'clock?"

"Nnooo," Trent groaned. "Maybe she'll go back to—"

"MAMA! TIME? DADDY!" Grace yelled from her room.

Maggie giggled, and it was music to his ears. If being exhausted eased the tension between them for just that day, it was worth feeling like he'd been run over by a huge toy truck. The absurd image of a toy truck chasing him down wrung a tired chuckle out of Trent.

"Well, it can't be too bad if you can laugh about it," Maggie said as she twisted her legs to sit atop the covers. Her cute flannel pajamas and sleep-mussed hair made her look more like a little girl than the sudden mother of four.

"I was just thinking I felt like I'd been run over by a toy truck, and I got this mental picture of an oversize toy truck chasing me around the house. Oh," he groaned, "I'm so tired I'm rambling. Please stop me next year if I get too carried away."

"What *did* you build?"

He listed what he could remember and added that there might be something he'd left out. It was Maggie's turn to start laughing. "Now I understand the sudden interest in the third floor. You have to fix up playrooms to put it all in? That's more work you've created for yourself!"

At that Trent howled with laughter. "I know. Which means Mickey following me every second he's home. I hope I live through more of his help."

Maggie, he could see, was trying hard to stay serious. "Trent, you're getting hysterical now. You're exhausted! You're taking a long nap before church. We'll go to the late service."

Trent took a deep breath, holding his aching side. He knew this was a release of tension, coupled with exhaustion, but it felt good to laugh with her and see her still concerned for him. "I'll take a nap like a good boy, Mommy," he choked, and started laughing again when she scowled.

"MAMA! DADDY!"

"Hey, you guys, how are we supposed to sleep?" Daniel groused outside their door. "Can I come in?"

Maggie pulled on her robe and climbed back under the covers. "Come on," she called.

"C'mon!" Mickey complained as he followed Daniel into the room. "I know you guys are new at this parent stuff but don't you know it's supposed to be us waking you guys up on Christmas morning. It's tradition. And you're supposed to complain that it's too early and you're tired."

"Mama! Daddy!" Grace screamed, clearly out of patience.

Deadpan, Maggie looked at Mickey and Daniel as Rachel stumbled in all sleepy-eyed and yawning. "It's too early. Uncle Trent is very tired," Maggie said to satisfy their craving for tradition.

Then Rachel, innocent that she was, added the killer punch to his aching stomach. "Then why's he laughing so loud that he woke us all up?"

And the whole absurd scene was too much for Trent's lost self-control. He went off again, laughing so hard he almost fell off the bed. The kids all looked at him as if he'd lost his mind, which made him laugh harder.

"Come on, kids. Let's leave this crazy man alone for a few minutes." She clapped her hands. "Everybody. Teeth brushed. Robes and slippers on. Meet in Grace's room. I'll be doing, hopefully, dry-diaper duty in there. And you—" she pointed to Trent "—light the tree and put on the carols."

Ten minutes later, the tree lights shining, Christmas carols in the air, they all went into the living room together. And the kids went crazy over their "Santa gifts." Trent and Maggie were both dragged from one gift to the next, and Trent had to pretend to "ooh" and "aah" over everything he'd spent so many hours making.

He'd never felt such satisfaction. Watching the joy his work brought to their precious faces was better than that first job—the infamous water heater—so many months earlier. They were awed and appreciative and already planning how to thank Santa. And he'd never loved them more, these children of his heart.

Mickey sidled over to him. "Thanks for the workbench and tools, Uncle Trent. Now I can help you even better."

"What happened to Santa?" he whispered back.

"I sort of figured out that he's pretend. But Aunt Maggie was so into taking us to see him at the mall and getting our pictures taken with him that I didn't want to wreck it for her. I had to pretend for the little ones anyway, so I just let Aunt Mag have her fun, too. She never got to play Mrs. Santa before, you know. And you never got to play Santa before either. But I wanted to thank you for the tool bench and stuff. You know?"

Trent ruffled Mickey's blond hair. "Yeah, kiddo, I understand. And thanks. Playing Santa was fun."

Mickey studied his face. "Then how come you look so tired?"

"Because Santa stays up all night Christmas Eve," Trent confided. "You get what I mean?"

Mickey nodded sagely. Clearly he did.

With Maggie around there was more to Christmas than Santa and the gifts he'd left. "Okay. Let's all sit over here on the sofa," she announced after they'd all played and admired the gifts Santa's elves had built. "I think before we open our family gifts, we should remember what this day's all about. Mickey, tell me about how the Christmas story starts."

"An angel appeared to Mary and told her God the Father wanted her to be the mother of His Son. And she said sure, since He was God and He was nice enough to send an angel to ask her and all. And then the angel told Joseph and he said cool, he'd be glad to be Jesus's guardian, sort of like you, Uncle Trent."

"Well, thanks, kiddo. I didn't know I was in such illustrious company as Saint Joseph," Trent said.

"Does anybody remember where that happened?" Maggie asked.

"In Narbeth!" Daniel shouted.

"Nazareth," Rachel corrected. "Narbeth is the town near Ardmore. But Jesus wasn't born in Nazareth 'cause the king who owned the world wanted to count all the people so he could charge them more taxes. Joseph had to take Mary to Bethlehem where people knew how to count."

Trent bit back a smile as Daniel's head bobbed in agreement. Mickey, he saw, was not as convinced that Bethlehem had been the counting capital of the world back then. Trent felt his heart swell. There was something so completely wonderful about four children listening so intently to the story of that first Christmas. It struck him as ironic that everything had been so much harder for the One all the celebration was supposed to honor than it was for so many of those He came to serve.

"Yeah," Daniel put in, agreeing with Rachel's

math theory. "And when they got to Bethlehem all the other people got there ahead of them. That was 'cause Mary couldn't walk so fast anymore, and they beat them there. So since they got there late there was no rooms to rent at any of the hotels or motels. Then a man felt sorry for their poor donkey 'cause Joseph stuck Mary on him when she couldn't keep up. But she was pretty fat by then and the donkey looked real tired. The nice man let Mary and Joseph sleep in his stable with their donkey, so he wouldn't be lonely."

Trent was fighting another fit of the giggles when Mickey jumped back in, preserving the authenticity of the actual birth record. "So Jesus was born that night and angels appeared to the shepherds who were watching their sheep in the fields. They told them all about how the Savior was born and that His name was Christ the Lord."

"They had baby lambs," Grace shouted, popping up like a jack-in-the-box to point at the manger. Then she just as quickly sat back down. "They taked one to Jesus to play with," she added, hugging her bear.

"That was after they got off the ground. They were down there because the angels really really scared them," Mickey continued.

"I think they got hurt, too, when they fell on the ground," Rachel added, "because they were sore and afraid."

"Yeah. Sore and afraid," Daniel agreed with a wise nod. "I remember that part, too!"

Shaking his head, Mickey jumped in again. "Then three kings were following a star and they got a little lost and stopped to ask directions on how to find Jesus. They were kings so they had to ask another king where they had to go. But he was a bad king and he killed all the little kids in Bethlehem later on but—'' Mickey sighed, out of breath ''—that's another story.''

Trent breathed a sigh of his own. He had enjoyed that and had managed not to laugh at the mixed-up rendition of the oft-told tale. He leaned back in the sofa as Grace crawled up into his lap.

''Do you all realize that the first Christmas was Jesus Christ's first sacrifice for us in a life full of sacrifices? And he became a little, helpless child that night. Look at Grace. Can you imagine going from just thinking something as huge as the world into existence to being as dependent on the people He created as Grace is on all of us?'' Maggie added a lesson that struck Trent with a sense of wonder. It was a side of the Christmas story he'd never considered.

''Uh-uh,'' they all said, shaking their heads. Their nearly identical brown eyes looked so serious and affected by her words that Trent felt compelled to look deeper than the traditional story and consider what Maggie had said.

Jesus Christ really *had* given up a lot. He'd cut off communications with His Father and was separate from Him for the first time. How frightening that must have been, to be so alone and isolated. And helpless. Why would He do that?

''I think He did it 'cause He loves us,'' Rachel said thoughtfully. ''I think He loves us an awful lot. He must have missed his daddy in heaven as much as we miss our mommy and daddy who are there now.

Maybe more, 'cause He was the one who had to go to the new place as a baby. At least we have you and Uncle Trent, and we knew both of you our whole lifes."

"You know, Rachel, I'm not sure I ever thought of it like that, but I bet you're right," Maggie said. "He must have missed His Father just as much as all of you miss yours. And you're right. He did it because He loves us. Now let's open the rest of our gifts and try to remember the gift He gave us almost two thousand years ago."

Trent sat up, bouncing Grace on his knee, and watched in awe as the children opened their gifts one at a time, helping Grace with her packages. There was wonder and sharing, gratitude and love shining on each sweet face. Choked up, he looked away and stared into the crèche that sat up on the mantel in a place of honor.

Christmas *was* about gifts. Grace. Salvation. Peace. And they all stem from His great love for us. Trent understood at last that all he had to do was reach out and take that gift the way the children did every time Maggie pulled one from under the tree and called out a name.

Blinking back tears, he closed his eyes. *Give me Your gifts, Jesus,* he prayed, *And You can have my life.*

Trent felt Maggie's hand on his shoulder. He looked up at her blurred form. "Tell me," she said, and wiped tears off his cheeks that he hadn't even realized he'd shed.

"After the court hearing, when I spoke to my

mother, she told me the truth about my parents, and everything I'd always believed fell apart. Which is one of the reasons I buried myself out at the workshop these last two nights. I think better while I'm working. And I've been doing a lot of thinking—and not just because you ordered me to later that night.'' He smiled and Maggie smiled back, warming his heart with the love shining in her eyes. For the first time he believed that everything was going to be all right.

''She also said my father was so proud of me that he insisted they keep my adoption secret. I realized that I didn't know anymore what was truth and what I'd fabricated out of hurt feelings. I've finally come to understand that they're just human and they made mistakes. Their views are skewed, but they aren't the monsters I'd blown them up to be either.''

''What did Albertine tell you about your parents?''

''That they were dead. It was an auto accident that killed them. Their names were James and Kathleen Trenton. I was named for their surname. James died instantly, and Kathleen died after I was born.

''Hearing that they'd loved me, that my mother's last act was to ask that my name be Trenton, meant so much. Then later in the evening, you came out to the workshop and it shook me when you told me that you'd love me no matter what, but that I had to decide what kind of marriage we'd have. Finally this morning, hearing the Christmas story and what you said about His sacrifices and why He made them, cemented it all together in my mind.

''I realized that God loves me and He confirmed

that love in my heart. I was so bitter and feeling so unloved that I couldn't see it before, I guess.''

Maggie finger-combed his hair gently and smiled. "I'm glad you finally know the truth. I know it's made you feel so much better about a lot of things."

"Having your forgiveness would make me feel even better. I'm sorry I didn't trust your love, Mag. Because I've loved you practically from the first moment I met you. I need you to understand that my heart was scarred for years by a secret shame that I was afraid to tell you about."

"Trent, what could you possibly have been so ashamed of. The adoption?"

Trent shook his head. How to explain? "You can't know what a life without love is like, Mag. You just can't know. I watch you with the kids. The little touches. The pats on their heads. The little smiles when they do some inconsequential thing right. All the little ways you show love. That's what drew me to you in the first place. I was like a man who'd been without water in the desert. I just lapped up all the love and affection that you gave. Because I'd never had that.

"Can you imagine hearing your parents discuss sending you away at age twelve as if you were an employee they'd decided to transfer? No emotion. No love. No loss. Then they start discussing the fact that you aren't even their child. So here were my parents, who clearly didn't love me, sending me away and being relieved because I made Mike look bad. Then I realized that my real parents obviously hadn't wanted me either.

"I thought 'What's wrong with me?' I spent hours that summer staring into the mirror, wondering what it was that they saw in me that I didn't. And I was still wondering the day I met you. I was still wondering when I went to bed last night.

"When you came into my life, I was instantly crazy about you. Then, like some dream come true, you loved me back. I couldn't stand to lose that, so I tried to be the person I thought you saw in me. And I still thought I was doing that. Even when I let you go, I told myself it was better that you left over not having children than that you saw it—the thing in me that repulsed two sets of parents."

"Oh, Trent," Maggie said, tears flooding her beautiful eyes.

"Shh," he whispered, and put his finger to her lips. "Don't cry, Maggie. It's all fine now. In court I knew I had to save those kids even if it meant smashing that facade. But these last two days I've gone over and over our relationship, and I realized there was no longer a facade between us anyway. I'd let it fade away years ago.

"The last vestige of my secret self—for want of a better description—was holding back the truth about my parents. I did it because I was afraid you'd see my great flaw if I let you know it was there. And, of course, once you knew it was there, you'd find it."

"So that's why you didn't tell me? Because you thought there was something wrong with you?" Her tone was incredulous.

Trent shrugged and felt a sheepish smile form on his lips. "Stupid, huh?"

Maggie shook her head. "Sad. Tragic. But not stupid. It just goes to prove how easily children can be damaged."

"But it proves something else, too. It proves how much Jesus can heal if we let Him. I feel like a new person already. He's filled all the empty places in my heart that I tried for so long to hide." He leaned forward and kissed her softly. "I don't want any more walls between us, Mag."

The sound of three childish sets of giggles drew their attention. Mickey knelt on the back of the sofa, holding a plastic mistletoe ball over their heads.

"Family hugs and kisses," Rachel called from her perch on the arm of the sofa, and Daniel shouted a lusty "Merry Christmas!" from his newly attained roost up next to Mickey. Then the three little bodies from above tackled Trent and Maggie, adding wild sloppy kisses to sweeten the family hug even more. Grace got into the act by planting a big wet baby kiss on Trent's cheek before giggling and diving for Maggie.

Trent closed his eyes. This was love. And that's what Christmas was all about.

Hours later the prediction Maggie made the night before the custody hearing had come true. They were both that wonderful kind of exhausted that only came after a day when there had been overwhelming joy— overwhelming love. Toys were scattered from one end of the usually neat living room to the other. All four energy-charged children were indeed safely tucked in their beds. And both Trent and Maggie were too tired to even consider the long climb up the stairs to their own room.

Maggie watched Trent push himself off the sofa and onto the floor. "I thought you were too tired to move," she said, then yawned expansively.

Trent sent her a spine-tingling grin. "I am, but I have one more thing to do," he replied, his voice full of lazy satisfaction.

"The children are all tucked in bed. The dishes are done. The Christmas lights are lit outside and on our perfect Christmas tree inside. What else could you possibly need to do?"

Trent winked, then crawled across the short distance to the tree. He reached way under, emerging a second later with a triumphant smile. Then he scrambled back over to her, a large square package in one hand. "This morning was for the kids. So I waited 'til now to give you this."

Maggie smiled lazily and took a sip of her tea. "I never gave you yours either." She pulled a flat box out from behind the pillow of the sofa. "But when *I* sat down, it was for the duration. I came prepared. Here's yours. Open it first."

Trent put his box down and accepted the gift. He tore the packaging off, every sign of exhaustion gone. The man just loved Christmas! She hoped he felt the same way about the leather-bound Bible.

He looked up, and his shining eyes gave her her answer. "How did you know I'd need this after today?"

Maggie reached out and covered his hand where it rested on the Bible. "I prayed. I hoped." She shrugged and grinned. "I prayed some more. Oh, Trent, Michael would be so pleased."

Trent nodded and extended the gift he had for her. "Thanks, Maggie. For the prayers and the patience. And for the chance to see Mike again."

Maggie smiled as she accepted the neatly wrapped package with the bright golden ribbon, but she shook her head. "I had very little to do with your decision. You may have started questioning the idea of faith because of the things I said, but it was ultimately between you and the Lord. It was His decision to knock, and yours to answer by accepting Him."

When she looked back at the package in her lap, she didn't know where she'd get the strength to tear off the wrapping. But a childlike enthusiasm welled up in her, bolstering her flagging energy. Soon she'd reduced the wrapping to a torn mass and pawed open the box. Inside was an identically wrapped box. She shot him a quelling glance. "We were in a mischievous mood while wrapping, weren't we?"

Trent replied with a boyish grin and a shrug.

The game of wrapped square box inside wrapped square box continued until she was down to one that was about four by four. Inside that one was a hand-blown concave Christmas ball. And nestled inside the spun-glass ornament was a tiny sleigh on a bed of cottony snow. And tucked in the back of the sleigh, behind a miniature Santa, was a diamond wedding band. "Oh, Trent," Maggie breathed. "It's so beautiful."

Trent took the ring carefully from its hiding place and reached for her left hand. As he removed her plain gold band and replaced it with the new one, he explained that the design had a special meaning. "The jeweler said the continuous band of stones symbolizes eternity. That's how long I'm going to love you, Mag. Into eternity. Just the way you love me."

Maggie blinked back sentimental tears as Trent went on. "This Christmas was so much more than I'd hoped, and the complete opposite of what I once dreaded. Six months ago I thought the end of this year was going to be the beginning of the rest of a lonely life. We were supposed to be divorced by now, and I couldn't imagine living the rest of my life without you, even though I was determined to do it.

"Instead, I got Christ, eternity, you back in my life and a family for Christmas. Merry Christmas, Maggie. Merry Christmas."

* * * * *

Dear Reader,

At the start of *A Family for Christmas* things looked pretty grim for the Osborne family. I've seen lives, including my own, look just as grim at times. But all we have to do is ask God for peace and strength, and He gives it in abundance. Just ask. How much more would our Heavenly Father give us? How much more perfect is His love?

The Lord often takes what looks like an impossible situation and finds a solution that is so miraculous that we can't believe the untold happiness that can result from those stressful times. Maggie found herself in just such a situation, and though she was a new believer, and though she occasionally forgot to turn to the Lord and became discouraged, when she remembered where to look for help, He was always there for her. He is there for all of us.

Maggie drew her strength and peace from the Lord in such an unmistakable way that Trent couldn't help noticing. Her quiet witness was enough to light the way for her husband to follow.

A Family for Christmas started out as a book about God's gifts. But it turned out to have almost as many lessons as it did children. I hope it reminds you this holy season of all the things God has given us. Especially the most precious gift of all—His Son.

Have a blessed Christmas and a safe and joyous New Year!

Kate Welsh

Take 2 inspirational love stories FREE!

PLUS get a FREE surprise gift!

Special Limited-Time Offer

Mail to Steeple Hill Reader Service™

In U.S.	In Canada
3010 Walden Ave.	P.O. Box 609
P.O. Box 1867	Fort Erie, Ontario
Buffalo, NY 14240-1867	L2A 5X3

YES! Please send me 2 free Love Inspired® novels and my free surprise gift. Then send me 3 brand-new novels every month, which I will receive months before they appear in bookstores. Bill me at the low price of $3.74 each in the U.S. and $3.96 each in Canada, plus 25¢ delivery and applicable sales tax, if any*. That's the complete price and a saving of over 10% off the cover prices—quite a bargain! I understand that accepting the books and gift places me under no obligation ever to buy any books. I can always return a shipment and cancel at any time. Even if I never buy another book from Steeple Hill, the 2 free books and the surprise gift are mine to keep forever.

303 IEN CM6R
103 IEN CM6Q

Name	(PLEASE PRINT)	
Address		Apt. No.
City	State/Prov.	Zip/Postal Code

* Terms and prices are subject to change without notice. Sales tax applicable in New York. Canadian residents will be charged applicable provincial taxes and GST. All orders subject to approval. Offer limited to one per household.

INTLI-299   ©1998